Out of Bounds

Out of Bounds

Sylvia Gunnery

James Lorimer & Company Ltd., Publishers
Toronto

© 2004 Sylvia Gunnery

James Lorimer & Company Ltd. acknowledges the support of the Ontario Arts Council. We acknowledge the support of the Government of Canada through the Book Publishing Industry Development Program (BPIDP) for our publishing activities. We acknowledge the support of the Canada Council for the Arts for our publishing program. We acknowledge the support of the Government of Ontario through the Ontario Media Development Corporation's Ontario Book Initiative.

Cover illustration: Greg Ruhl

The Canada Council   Le Conseil des Arts
for the Arts   du Canada

ONTARIO ARTS COUNCIL
CONSEIL DES ARTS DE L'ONTARIO

Canada Cataloguing in Publication Data

Gunnery, Sylvia
  Out of bounds / written by Sylvia Gunnery.

(Sports stories ; 70)
ISBN 1-55028-827-X (bound)   ISBN 1-55028-826-1 (pbk.)

I. Title. II. Series: Sports stories (Toronto, Ont.); 70.

PS8563.U575O98 2004   jC813'.54   C2004-900483-2

James Lorimer & Company Ltd.,   Distributed in the United States by:
Publishers   Orca Book Publishers
35 Britain Street   P.O. Box 468
Toronto, Ontario   Custer, WA USA
M5A 1R7   98240-0468
www.lorimer.ca

Printed and bound in Canada.

Contents

1	Rockets Rule!	9
2	Thin Ice	19
3	Fire!	26
4	Counter-Clockwise	36
5	Caution	44
6	Disappearing	54
7	Hitchhiking to Nowhere	63
8	Changing Colours	72
9	Out of Bounds	81
10	Courage	90

Acknowledgements

I acknowledge, with thanks, the generous advice of Darren Haley and Rhonda Himmelman, basketball coaches at Hebbville Academy in Lunenburg County, Nova Scotia.

For Jim

1

Rockets Rule!

The time on the scoreboard blinked red, high in the corner of the gymnasium: 1:03. Jay knew how quickly a minute of basketball could disappear, evaporate into a sudden blast of the buzzer to end the game. He had the ball. The score was 79–77 for the Centreville Cougars. Jay could feel all the hopes of the Richmond Rockets fans pressing down on him.

He beat the Centreville guard easily with a crossover move and willed his long legs to carry him to that precious point to the right of the basket. There he suddenly stopped, as he had hundreds of times in practice. He balanced and concentrated, with just enough time to bend his knees and leap, sending the ball in an arc towards the basket, following through with his right arm, letting his wrist drop like a final exclamation mark. In! 79–79!

But as his body descended, the forearm of his opponent struck the side of his head. It felt like a baseball bat in full swing. Jay collapsed on the floor, and for a shadow of a second thought absurdly of floor polish before everything around him blurred.

He barely remembered the medic checking his neck, his pulse, his eyes. He barely remembered being carried off the floor on a stretcher while his opponent in the red and yellow jersey ran along beside him.

Jay blinked and then opened his eyes. His coach said, "There's our man. There's our man. How's she goin', Jay? Got yer legs back yet?"

"What's the final score?" he asked.

"Score? There is no final score. The clock's stopped while we wait for you to take a nap. Fine time to take a nap, if ya ask me." Then Coach Willis turned to the medic and said, "Let's get this player back on the bench so's he can watch his team win this game."

"He's gonna be okay, then, eh?" The voice of the player in the red and yellow jersey was deep, and there was a hesitation in his question.

Jay looked over at his opponent standing behind the medic and Coach Willis. He was tall and narrow with thick black hair, his brown eyes frowning. Mike Murphy. The Cougars' starting centre. Number 10. Tallest guy in the whole league. Jay had jumped against him lots of times since basketball season had begun in November.

"He'll have a headache. But other than that, he'll be fine," said the medic.

Then the red and yellow jersey was gone.

When Jay came back into the gymnasium, voices screamed: *Jay! Jay! Jay! Jay!*

He lifted his hand in a weak salute and tried not to look as if he really did need to lean against Coach Willis. Taking high-fives from everyone he passed, he made his way to the space cleared for him on the bench. It was a relief to fold his five-foot seven-inch frame into a sitting position and lean his elbows on his knees. He ran his fingers through the long strands of brown hair that fell across one side of his forehead.

The time on the scoreboard now read 11 seconds.

Colin, wearing the Rockets jersey number 36, would take

the foul shot since Jay was officially out of this game. Last year, Jay's best friend Colin had won MVP for Richmond Academy. Everyone hushed so he could show them once again how valuable he really was to his team, to his school.

The players positioned themselves along the key, elbows out, knees bent, ready to make the last seconds of this basketball game count big.

Silence. Colin bounced the ball three times. Taking a deep breath, he pushed all his concentration into the direction of that basketball. Up and up and up. Then down and down and in! 79–80!

Cheers exploded from the Richmond fans.

Eight seconds remained in the game. A Centreville player took the ball outside the court under the basket. His quick outlet pass to the point guard zapped past the Richmond Academy players, who were caught up in the expectation of winning and caught off guard by the determination of Centreville's team. The next pass landed the ball in Murphy's hands.

Murphy ran down the outside lane, alone, unstoppable. He must have seen the clock: five seconds left. With all the force of a shot putter, Murphy hefted the basketball from centre court — his only chance for those precious points.

The buzzer blasted! The ball was still in the air. Silence sucked all the oxygen from the gymnasium. Going, going, going. It hit the rim. Like a boomerang, the ball was coming back into the court. The game was over before it hit the floor.

Centreville 79, Richmond Academy 80! The impossible had been achieved — Centreville, always victorious over Richmond Academy and holding the Western Region Boys Junior Basketball Championship for three years straight, had finally been defeated.

Everything was now possible.

* * *

Outside, the bleak January night was dotted with snow flurries and the wind gusted as players and fans rushed to cars, vans, and trucks idling in the schoolyard of Richmond Academy. Nova Scotia was breaking two records: the lowest temperature in ten years (minus twenty-one Celsius) and the greatest January snowfall since Jay was born thirteen years ago (sixty-two centimeters). The river running through the town of Richmond was clogged with large pans of ice floating slowly down towards the sea twenty kilometers south.

The Centreville bus was pulling out of the driveway and a few Richmond fans were jeering, "Go home, losers!"

Jay had a grin on his face, listening to the jeers and knowing he had played his part well in Centreville's defeat. After only two years in this basketball league, his reputation was solid. The fans could count on number 27: his height, his speed, his bull's-eye accuracy, and his strong sense of team spirit.

Then he thought about after the game, when the teams had lined up to shake hands or give a high five, and how Murphy had made a fist and tapped Jay lightly on his arm. The move had made Jay flinch. "Hope you don't have much of a headache or anything," Murphy had said. Because the guys behind him were moving the line along, Jay had no time to respond.

Coach Willis was leaning into the van, explaining the blackout incident to Jay's father. "Ah, ya can't stop this guy. He's got a noggin on him like a boulder. But all the same, it'd be good to keep an eye on him for the next twenty-four. He can take it easy tomorrow, seeing as it's Saturday."

Jay climbed into the front seat. Behind him sat his younger brother, Sam, who was five, and their German Shepherd, Rudy.

"Thanks Ed," said Jay's father. "I'll make sure Jay calls you tomorrow with a full health report. He'll be fine. If he's anything like me, those two points were worth a slam on the noggin."

"Like in the '85 Regionals. You played like a crazy man, Brian. Like a crazy man." Coach Willis scratched his head as if trying to uncover a few lost details in his memory. "Well, take it easy then. Take it easy."

"Will do."

Rudy was licking Jay's ear and Sam was stretching forward to feel the bump on Jay's head. "Cut it out. Both of you. Geez."

"What do you guys say to some grease on a bun and some frics before we pick Mom up?" said Mr. Hirtle.

Later, as they waited in front of the hospital for Jay's mother to finish her shift on emergency, Jay could feel the headache taking possession of his skull. He realized, too, that he was dreading the third degree he'd get from his mother and the once-over with half the instruments in her medical bag. All his life, if something happened and his mom was there, she would downplay her concern. But if she missed out on the accident, she had to know every single insignificant detail. Was it the arm or the elbow that hit you? Was it the top of your head or the back? Did you see silver spots when you passed out? What colour was your underwear?

There she was now, buttoning her coat as she opened the hospital door, her long yellow scarf whipped by the wind like two crazy arms. She wore a yellow toque pulled down over her eyebrows.

Jay got out and jumped into the back seat with Sam and Rudy.

She kissed her husband with a loud, "Mmmmmmm!" for the benefit of the back-seat audience.

Rudy was practically leaping into the front to welcome his

favourite person in the whole family: the one who had picked him and his sad eyes out of all the other puppies at the animal shelter, the one who fed him and walked him every single day, the one who would move her feet on the sofa to make room for him as she read her book.

"And how are all the important men in my life tonight? How was the game, Jay?"

"We beat Centreville. Finally. I tied the score just about at the end of the game."

"Jay had a con-cushion," said Sam.

"Concussion," corrected his father.

"A concussion! What are you saying?"

"It wasn't a concussion, Mom. Just a little bump on the head. Sam, I'm gonna have to report you to the vocabulary police. Seriously. Con-cushion. Now look, you got Mom all tied in a knot."

"We'll check you over thoroughly when we get home." She slipped the seatbelt over her shoulder and snapped it into place.

"White and blue," said Jay.

"What? White and blue what?" his mother asked.

"Underwear."

"Huh?"

"Nothing, Mom. Just a private joke."

"White and blue underwears," said Sam to Rudy.

"Congrats on the win, sweetheart. That's super-dooper double-time."

"Thanks, Mom."

"Super-pooper," Sam was saying, probably to Rudy, but maybe not.

"Did you have time to pick up groceries, Brian?" Jay's mother asked.

"Did so."

"Did you feed this carload of mouths?"

"Did so."

"That's my man," she said, rubbing his earlobe playfully.

Jay took note. His dad obviously liked that move. He was giving her one of those smiles where one eyebrow goes up and the corner of the mouth does too. Jay was wondering whether that earlobe thing would work the other way around, guy to girl.

Sam never noticed these things. So far, it looked to Jay as if Sam wasn't in training for anything. Just living inside his own world, repeating and mispronouncing the occasional word more because he liked the sound of it than because he planned to use it in any kind of sensible way. Like last night when Sam had watched his mother put the white mounds of meringue on top of a lemon pie, he kept saying, "Lemon merango pie. Lemon merango pie," even though he knew that wasn't the right word at all. Sam probably drove his teacher nuts.

Rudy, however, did notice the earlobe move. He pushed his big head forward and offered his own ear for the same treatment. He got it and moaned slightly. This was encouraging to Jay, who was figuring that it might work guy to girl if it worked mom to dad and then mom to dog. He started daydreaming about the right place, the right time he could give that move a try.

* * *

The next afternoon, after his mother was satisfied that Jay's skull wasn't significantly altered and when she and Sam and Rudy were out for a walk, the telephone rang.

"Got it!" yelled Jay. "Hello."

"How long's a guy supposed to wait around for that health report?"

"Oh geez, Coach. I forgot. Sorry."

"You got some kind of brain damage or what?"

Jay meant to laugh, but he snorted into the telephone, like a cartoon pig. "No, it's not brain damage. I'm fine. Mom checked me over. All I got is a bump on the head."

"Good, then. Can't have our starting centre sitting on the bench with brain damage all season."

He pictured Coach Willis grinning at his own joke, his face all folded up under the eyes and at the corners of his mouth. His grey hair was just a bit too long at the back, maybe to make up for the empty space on the top of his head.

"Thanks for the call, Coach. See you at school."

"Right."

Jay walked over to the kitchen window and looked out into the backyard where snowdrifts had piled up along the picket fence, leaving the tops exposed like a row of green teeth. A neighbour's black cat was tiptoeing across the teeth. Two chickadees were darting to a feeder and then back into the thick branches of a spruce tree. The cat was heading in the direction of the feeder.

Jay went back to the phone and dialed.

"Hey, Colin. What's up?"

"Nothin'. You?"

"Nothin'." He sat down on the floor and leaned against the kitchen wall. "Pretty good game. Your last point was gold."

"What about that Murphy?" said Colin. His words sounded like a threat.

"What about him?"

"I can't stand him. It's like he's some kind of phony, or something."

Jay was looking down at his sneakers. They looked exactly like his grandfather described them: shoeboxes stuck at the ends of two long oars. "What makes you think Murphy's a phony?"

"It's just his atmosphere. Like when he hit you, there he was chasing after the stretcher like some kind of 911 guy. And I saw the look on his face when he came back out of the locker room. He had this big, stupid grin like he was so happy he took out one of our players. I hate the guy."

"Yeah, well, he's opponent number one. If we stop Murphy, we stop Centreville. Just like we did yesterday."

"Right. Centreville's a bunch of hicks anyway."

There was his grandfather again. Jay had a sudden memory of the old man walking out to his lopsided fish shack that stood on stilts at the end of that wonky old wharf. At seventy-eight, Gramp still followed a few routines from his lobster fishing days: up early, checking the tides and marine weather, winding and rewinding long lengths of rope. But he was left behind, now, when the boats left the channel. Centreville Channel.

"That bunch of Centreville hicks don't stand a chance. Not even with that beanpole Murphy. They're probably all sitting around cryin' like babies because they had to take a loss."

"They better get used to it. The Rockets rule."

"It's like we already own that championship banner. The Cougars are such losers."

Jay could picture the Richmond Academy team photograph that would be taken after the championship game. Coach Willis would be standing at one end of the middle row, his hands behind his back, wearing his white and blue coach's shirt. Jay and Colin would be in the centre of the middle row, holding the top corners of the championship banner. Some guys would be kneeling on one knee. Some guys would be standing just like Coach. *Click*. The centrefold for Richmond's yearbook.

"So, you doing anything tonight?"

"Told Mom and Dad I'd babysit Sam."

"Tough break."

"What're you doin'?"

"Nothin'. It's too damn cold to go anywhere. Man, I'll be glad when I get my license."

"That's three more years."

"Two and three-quarters."

"Yeah, well don't hold your breath. Anyway, talk to ya later."

"Right."

Jay got up from the floor and put the receiver on its hook. He was thinking about Colin, about how sometimes you think you know a guy because you've been going to the same school since you were both five. But suddenly, the guy starts being different. Weird different. Like just now, when Colin kept going on and on about Centreville hicks and about hating Mike Murphy.

Three-ten. Nothing to do. Jay walked over to the fridge, lifted out the orange juice carton, removed the round green cap, and took a long gulp.

He went back to the phone again, slid down the wall to sit on the floor, and dialed.

"Hello?"

There, just like that, Allie's voice in his ear. Allie's soft, sure, turquoise-coloured, sexy voice.

"Hi. It's me."

"Hi."

2

Thin Ice

In the next few basketball games, the Richmond Rockets brought home two wins and had only one loss:

Richmond Academy 56, Lakeview Consolidated 52.

Richmond Academy 50, Dr. A. C. MacLeod 46.

Lakeview Consolidated 57, Richmond Academy 54.

At practice after that loss to Lakeview, Coach Willis seemed to have a gap in his memory when it came to the games Richmond had won. All he could think of to say in his pep talk was stuff like, "Lakeview's got your number," or, "Maybe we should just hand the banner over to Lakeview this year." If anyone ever told Coach Willis about the power of positive thinking, he hadn't paid any attention.

Colin sat on the bench in the locker room and leaned against the white-tiled wall. His hair was stuck to his forehead as if he'd just surfaced from a dive into a pool. Droplets of sweat were running like water down his neck. "Nothin' went right today," he complained to Jay. "It's like my hands were allergic to the damn ball."

"It's only practice."

"But practice is how I get psyched up. Like, if things go smooth, I know they'll go smooth in the next game. Kind of like an omen."

"Omens aren't real."

"Right," said Colin sarcastically. "So why do you always wear those stupid white and blue boxers at every freakin' game? With all those squares and circles on them? Bet you don't even wash them. The stink'd mean even better luck."

"Get real." Jay sure wasn't about to tell Colin that he had sewn up a rip along the waistband of those old boxers or that he'd been searching for new white and blue ones in Harmon's Men's Wear down on King Street. "We'll be psyched for Centreville anyway. They'll be thinking about how we pounded their score down last time we played them."

"I'd like to pound that Murphy down," said Colin, getting up from the bench and picking up his towel.

There he was again, acting all weird about Murphy. Like Murphy was some kind of enemy, a soldier sneaking up on them through a muddy battlefield with a rifle ready to fire deadly rounds.

Jay couldn't think of anything to say that would come out right. Maybe before Friday's game against Centreville, Coach Willis might think of something positive to say to the team and Colin might forget about his allergic hands and about pounding Murphy.

* * *

Math class was adding up to more boredom than usual. Friday afternoon, last class, and an endless review of integers. Jay's pencil felt as heavy as an axe.

Finally, overhead, the hum and click of the PA system were heard. "Sorry for this interruption. Would teachers please excuse the members of the girls and boys basketball teams travelling to Centreville for today's competitions? Players are to meet in the front lobby. Thank you."

Jay met Colin in the hall and they headed to their lockers together. "Ready for another win?"

"Right!" said Colin. "And I hope Murphy's ready for another loss."

The girls game was first. But Richmond's fast pace and team spirit didn't threaten the Centreville girls team. The final score was Centreville 52, Richmond 44.

When the girls went back to the locker rooms and the boys took possession of the court, there was an electric tension in the air. The Centreville boys were sure they were going to follow the lead set by their girls team. The Richmond Academy boys were determined to even up the scoreboard with a victory.

Jay stood at centre, his body angled, ready for the jump to start the game. Murphy was in front of him, just on the other side of the referee. They had given the mandatory handshake without actually making eye contact. The noise of the crowd lowered to a babble and then to a hush.

The referee tossed the basketball into the air. Jay was up. Murphy was up. Their long arms reached high; their fingers tipped the ball at the same time. But Murphy had more force, and the basketball spun off towards a player in red and yellow.

Instantly, two players in white and blue became a fence in front of the Centreville player and they left no opened gate. He stopped, lifted the ball over his head, and looked for someone ready to receive it. The hesitation was just long enough for Richmond to tap it out of his hands.

The Rockets now had the ball. The players changed direction and ran towards the Centreville basket, collecting in a tangle on the left. Jay had taken his best position at the right of the key. There was a leap of white and blue out of the tangle and the ball drifted towards him.

Murphy came out of nowhere and intercepted. Centreville

ball. Everyone reversed momentum and raced after Murphy. He passed the centre line and scored an easy two points from the top of the key. Centreville 2, Richmond Academy 0.

Murphy's team swarmed him as if those first two points had won the game. They were psyched.

"Keep your heads up!" Coach Willis shouted from the bench.

Colin took the ball out of bounds. He bounced it in a sharp angle to the right and the referee's arm dropped to start the game time rolling again. Richmond was on its way down the court, heavily guarded by Centreville.

"Pass! Pass! Pass!" yelled Coach Willis. One inch closer to the edge of that bench and he'd slip right off.

Richmond passed the ball under the elbows of the guards and it continued its path down court towards the Centreville basket. Again, there was a tangle of players, then a double dribble. The ref's whistle blew and the ball was Centreville's again.

The inbounds pass went right to Murphy. His face was distorted with fierce determination as he swung around and aimed himself towards the Richmond basket. Jay caught up with him and smacked at the ball. Murphy kept going. Jay scrambled again, reaching to tip the ball as Murphy leaped to shoot. Jay's fingertips spun the ball off its course. It hit the rim of the basket and bounced high. Colin was up there like a rocket, grabbing the ball firmly and landing solidly on his two feet. Fake left, fake right, pass the ball out to Jay.

Jay was away from Richmond's territory in a split second, bouncing the ball with authority, glancing to the left to see Colin get ready for the return pass. With a blur of red and yellow jerseys right behind him, Jay made the long, safe pass to Colin.

Now Richmond was on Centreville's turf. Jay made a cut to the foul line. Back came the ball. Got it! Two guards blocked him as he pivoted forward, back, right. He sent the ball in a low straight line to Colin who was directly under the basket, ready. In what looked like one smooth motion, Colin caught the pass, leaped into the air, and dunked the ball through the hoop.

Score tied!

With only six minutes of the game gone, the players were red-faced and sweating with exertion and excitement. Each person on the basketball court and on the team benches was there for only one purpose: to win!

Richmond's score inched ahead, stalled, then recovered: two point lead, four-point lead, two-point lead, tied again, two-point lead. But when the buzzer went, the half-time score was Centreville Cougars 26, Richmond Rockets 22.

Music blared from the speakers. Some fans kicked off winter boots and slid in sock feet on the polished floor, grabbing a couple of basketballs and taking a few shots.

The players were sequestered in their locker rooms with towels to dry off the sweat running into their eyes, cold water to quench parched throats, and orange slices to pep up their energy. Their ears were filled with coaches' instructions: do this, remember that, watch out for this play, keep an eye on that player, and get the lead out!

"Colin, I want you right there under that basket to get every rebound. Make your hands like glue. Jay, get to that magic spot over on the right and be ready for the ball. Make every shot count. The rest of you guys get a picture of that basketball in your heads and keep it there. Think of nothin' else 'til we win this game."

Coach Willis' words stayed with the Richmond team as the game jumped into action in the second half. Each player on the court was alert with tension, every pair of eyes followed the ball, all the passes were clean, and each play was executed with precision. Richmond was ready to pass and race and leap their way to a second win against Centreville.

But what they were ready to do didn't happen. With seven minutes left in the game, Colin fouled Murphy as he took a shot.

It wasn't just that Colin fouled, though. He swore. Then he fought.

Murphy had been running smoothly along the outside lane, far ahead of all the other players except for Colin. Richmond was trying hard to keep the two-point lead they had gained. Murphy knew he could erase it. Colin kept trying to position himself between Murphy and the basket, but his opponent slipped ahead, then stopped to make his play. Colin leaped and pounded the basketball out of Murphy's hands. The ref's whistle screeched.

Coach Willis was up off the bench and shouting, "Where's your glasses, ref? Here, take mine!"

"What?" shouted Colin. "That was clean! That was clean! I didn't even touch the guy!" Then he said a four-letter word. If he could have just picked any other four letters to spit out of his mouth, it wouldn't have been so bad. But at that moment, the alphabet was against him, and Colin muttered the familiar four-letter word at the referee.

"Technical foul, number 36!"

Murphy would get two foul shots, standing at the key alone, almost guaranteed double points.

That's when Colin lost it. He shoved Murphy when he walked by on his way to the foul line. Murphy said something and Colin went after him, fists flying. The two players were held apart before any fists landed.

"Calm your player," said the referee to Coach Willis. "Get some control here."

Coach Willis signalled Colin to the bench and sent in a substitute.

Now the Richmond Rockets were rattled. Despite the best team effort they could muster, Centreville pushed ahead and won the game.

"What'd Murphy say?" asked Jay when the team was on the bus and Coach Willis was muttering to himself in his seat behind the driver.

"Some jerk thing," said Colin. "I didn't hear exactly what."

"But—" Jay stopped for a couple of seconds, wanting to say this without adding more fuel to Colin's temper. "If you didn't hear what he said, why'd you bother going at the guy?"

"Just the way it sounded. Like some kind of put down. It got to me."

Jay looked out the bus window into the dark February evening. On this stretch of country road, the deep forest was uninterrupted on both sides until they came to the top of the hill where the town of Richmond could be seen as a cluster of lights in the next valley. There wasn't much sense saying anything more to Colin about the fight. Nothing would change what happened. Colin had completely lost it. Jay had never seen him explode like that. Lately, it was like there was thin ice over things Colin said and things he did. Then the ice would suddenly crack wide open. What was it about Murphy that could crack that ice?

3

Fire!

On Saturday afternoon, Colin showed up at Jay's, hunching his shoulders and trying to hide his ears inside the collar of his jacket. His bare hands were stuffed deep into his pockets.

"Hey, Colin. What's up? Come on in."

"Wanna do something?"

"Such as?"

"I dunno. Just hang out."

"You look like an ice cube."

"Over at the mall maybe."

Jay grabbed his heaviest jacket and his black toque. "Mom! Dad! I'm going over to the mall with Colin!" He was out the door before anyone answered him.

On the way to the mall, which was five blocks over, next to the LaHave River, they stopped twice to warm up: first at the drug store where they checked out magazines but didn't buy any, and second at the sports store where Colin tried on five pairs of basketball shoes even though he owned new ones already.

All the usual things were happening at the mall because it was Saturday and because it was freezing cold outside. Seniors were strolling around, clocking a couple of slow kilometers of exercise. Girls who had left their coats with friends who worked in some of the shops were walking in twos and threes, wearing jeans and scooped-necked, sleeveless T-shirts like it was the middle of July. Booths were set up where men from the YMCA or women from the church auxiliary were selling raffle tickets for cars or quilts. Some people were even shopping.

"Hey," said Colin suddenly, as if someone had bumped into him, "that's Murphy over there."

Jay thought about thin ice.

"What's he doing out of Hicksville?" said Colin. "Let's go find out."

"Who cares about Murphy?" said Jay, his words walking carefully, looking for cracks.

"I'm gonna check the situation."

Colin went towards Murphy. Jay didn't move. Murphy turned around, as if warned, just before Colin stepped up to him. Colin was talking, but Jay couldn't hear a thing. Then Murphy walked away. Colin reached out as if to grab Murphy, but either missed or changed his mind.

"That guy's asking for it." Colin was still looking in the direction Murphy had gone.

"Why? Did he say something?"

"He's a loser."

"He said he was a loser?"

"No, stupid."

Jay felt an uncomfortable twitch at the back of his neck. "What's with you?"

"He's the reason I got benched."

You're the one who hit him, not the other way around. You're the one who swore at the ref. "Look, I gotta go. I forgot I had to do something back home."

"What?"

"Just stuff. You stayin' here?"

"Nothing else to do."

"Yeah."

"Give me a call."

"Yeah. See ya."

When he left the mall, Jay didn't go directly home. First he warmed up again at the drug store and then went down the hill to Harmon's Men's Wear. It was his lucky day — they had the white and blue underwear. He bought two pairs. You never know when they'd have the right kind in stock again.

* * *

The retired couple that lived next door was standing in their driveway talking to Jay's mother as if it were a cocktail party and not a subzero wind-chill day. Then he remembered that they were planning to take a two-week vacation in the Dominican Republic. Lucky.

Mrs. Todd was saying something about leaving the thermostat for the electric heat turned low. Mr. Todd said they had cancelled the newspaper for the next two weeks.

"You have a wonderful time," Jay's mother said. "Don't worry a bit. Everything will be fine."

They got into their car and slowly backed out of the driveway, with Mrs. Todd at the wheel and Mr. Todd double-checking for something in his wallet.

Jay and his mother waved goodbye until the car turned left at the end of the street and was out of sight.

"Wouldn't mind being them," said Jay, hunching his shoulders against the cold wind. "They're lucky."

But that was before the fire.

* * *

That night, in the pitch black, Jay was startled awake by a loud crack — like a gunshot. It was the sudden sound of roof boards shrinking in the frigid outdoor temperatures. Even though this was happening a lot lately, it still woke him and sent his heart pounding until he realized where he was and what he'd heard. The green face of his bedside clock read 12:48. He had been in bed less than two hours.

Instantly, he was sleeping again.

From down the dark tunnel of his dreams, he heard Rudy barking and barking and barking. Then Jay was wide awake again and the dog was up on the bed, barking a frantic warning into his face.

Smoke! An orange glow stained the darkness outside his bedroom window.

"Hurry, Jay!" shouted his father. "Sam's with your mother! Grab your boots and coat in the front hall! Hurry! Come, Rudy. Good boy."

The fire engines were screaming from only blocks away as they all stood outside with dozens of neighbours, in awe, watching flames shoot out from under the eaves of the Todds' garage.

Firefighters took over, attacking the fire and moving the crowd back.

"We'll get you to move that van!" one firefighter shouted to Jay's father. "I'd say get your family inside somewhere, out of this cold."

"Right." He was mesmerized by the spectacle in front of him, realizing that the fiery garage was closer to their own home than it was to the Todds'.

Quickly, he backed the van out into the street. "Come on, everyone, get in," he said to his family. "I'm taking you over to Gramp's." Then, as they drove away from the fiery, crowded scene, he added, "They'll soon get things under control."

"Maybe we should just go across the street. Stay at Mac-Dougalls' until we can go back into our house." His mother had turned towards the back seat to rub her hand along Sam's knees reassuringly. Rudy licked her ears.

"Might take a while. Better let these guys get some sleep where there's peace and quiet. Give Dad a call, will you Dorothy? Let him know we're on the way and that everyone's okay."

From where Jay sat, he could see his mother's long flannel nightie under her winter coat. He leaned to peer around his father's seat and saw that he was still in his pajamas too. Although in other circumstances this might have struck Jay as comical, tonight it added to his fear. His heart was beating so hard the noise thumped in his ears.

Sam was sucking his thumb and staring straight ahead.

Rudy put his head down and whined.

"We're on the way over," his mom was saying into the cell phone. "The Todds' garage caught on fire. We had to evacuate … Yes, just to be on the safe side… Okay, Gramp. We'll be there soon."

Never before had Jay stood so close to a fire, a real one, not a campfire or a bonfire of fall leaves. It was almost as if those flames had been alive, with brains to think of ways to twist and turn and destroy. When the water from the fire hoses splashed against the garage roof, the flames would diminish and sputter, but only for a moment. Instantly, they jumped up and fought back.

One firefighter had shouted to another, "There's no car in that garage, but there's probably a snow blower. Maybe a lawn mower too. There'll be gas tanks."

It was like there were bombs in the garage, timed to explode. Maybe in a movie that'd be cool to watch, but in the middle of the night with the bombs right next to his own house,

Jay felt totally different. He was glad they were driving away from the fire.

* * *

The drive over to Gramp's in Centreville took forty minutes or fifty-five, depending on whether they went on the main highway or took the old road that curled in and out of each cove along the way. Tonight they were doing the forty-minute version of the trip. It wasn't snowing, but the wind was blowing snow around in places where there were open fields or open sea.

Gramp lived by himself. Jay barely remembered his grandmother, and Sam had never met her at all. Every time he went into that white saltbox-style house up on a small hill above the wharf, Jay had a strong feeling of someone missing. The house smelled different now, more like rubber boots and toast than like tea biscuits and hand cream.

"Here they are. Here they are," said the old man, opening the door and pushing it against the wind that gusted up from the channel. "Hi, fella," he said to Sam and patted his head. Then he patted Rudy's head in the same way.

"Hi, Dad," said Jay's father. "Sorry 'bout getting you up in the middle of the night like this."

"No trouble a'tall. What else am I here for? Hi there, Jay."

"Hi, Gramp." Jay shook his grandfather's hand and gave him a sideways hug at the same time.

"I made up your dad's old bed for you two boys. Want some milk, maybe some crackers and peanut butter, before you turn in?"

"I'll put on the kettle," said Jay's mom.

"Think I'd better drive back there," said his dad.

"Oh, they'll have that fire out by now. May as well just stay and get some sleep, now that you're here. All of you," said Gramp.

"Tomorrow's lots of time for going back home when all the fuss is over."

They settled around the kitchen table as if it were the middle of the day instead of the middle of the night. Sam was soon fast asleep in his father's arms.

"Better get this guy to bed. You coming up too, Jay?"

"Sure."

Jay had slept lots of times in his dad's old room, including a few Christmases he could hardly remember and some weekends after his grandmother died. It was an ordinary room with not too much left from the time before his father went to university. In fact, the room looked pretty empty: a bed, a bureau, a half-filled bookcase, and a round hooked mat on the floor.

There on the wall was the red and yellow Centreville school pennant, tacked sideways. In the yearbook on the bookshelf was a picture Jay had looked at dozens of times. His dad, wearing his red and yellow Centreville jersey, was in that picture, in the middle row holding one corner of the Junior Boys Regional Basketball Championship banner.

Weird, thought Jay. He remembered jumping for the tipoff against Mike Murphy. Murphy in the Cougar colours. His dad in the Cougar colours. Too weird.

Jay's father gently placed Sam down on the bed and rolled him towards the wall. "Enough room for you, do you think?"

"Yeah. It's okay."

"Pretty scary night. For all of us," said his dad.

"Yeah."

"Try to get some sleep. Want me to send Rudy upstairs?"

"Sure."

Later, when Jay and Rudy and Sam were sleeping like boulders tumbled together on the small bed, his dad drove back to Richmond, alone, unable to stay away.

* * *

The Hirtle family gathered around Gramp's kitchen table early the next morning. Jay's father was explaining how, by the time he had returned to the scene of the fire, the flames had won the battle against the fire department. Fire had leaped onto the back porch of the Hirtles' house and crawled hungrily upward.

"It'll be months before we can get back home,' said Jay's dad. He told Jay and Sam the basics about the destruction done by the fire: the back porch was destroyed, Jay's bedroom had been gutted, and there was a lot of smoke and water damage. But he didn't describe any vivid details. Everyone was upset enough without that right now.

"Plenty a room here for the whole lot a ya," said Gramp, who kept pacing the kitchen, making more toast and pouring more tea or milk.

Mrs. Hirtle was leaning on her elbows, rubbing the tension in her forehead. "Thanks, Gramp. What would we do without you?" She tried to smile at him as he put another slice of toast on her plate.

"We'll get some new plans drawn up for a nice large kitchen," said Jay's father. "With a window seat, just like we always wanted. And you can make all the decisions about what your new bedroom will be like, Jay. May as well see the bright side of all this."

"Who cares what a new bedroom looks like?" Jay knew his voice sounded a lot like Rudy's whining, but it was his bedroom that didn't exist anymore, his DVD player and computer, his posters, his old sneakers. Where was the bright side to that?

"Your mom and I've talked about how it's probably a good idea if you finish out the year over here at Centreville School. You and Sam. The school bus stops right down at the end of the lane."

"Centreville! Are you guys nuts! I can't switch schools! No way!"

"When you're ready to tone down that voice, Jason," said his mother sternly, "we will continue this conversation." She got up from the table, collecting some dirty dishes and taking them to the sink.

"I'll get those, Dorothy," said Gramp softly. "You go have a rest. Everyone's too tired today."

"I'm not going to Centreville! You can just forget about that stupid idea!" Jay pushed his chair back and ran upstairs, slamming the bedroom door behind him. For a moment he just stood there, fuming, wanting to cry and forcing himself not to. Then he walked over to the Centreville pennant hanging on the wall and pulled it roughly off. The tacks flew and landed soundlessly somewhere. He threw the pennant into the closet and slammed that door too.

* * *

On Monday, Jay's mother drove him over to Richmond Academy where they started the paperwork for the transfer. Allie already knew, of course, because she and Jay had talked on the phone for an hour, even though it was long distance and even though Gramp didn't have a long-distance phone plan.

When the bell rang to begin classes, Allie didn't let go of Jay's hand. "I'm not going to class," she said. They both felt as if Jay and his family were moving to the Yukon, not just down the road to Centreville.

Coach Willis came out of the staff room, holding a stack of photocopies, probably still warm. Jay didn't know what to say, but Coach Willis wasn't lost for words. "We're all pretty upset about what happened there, Jay. Bad luck. Pure bad luck. But no one was hurt. There's the thing to be grateful for. Mighty, mighty grateful."

"Thanks, Coach." Jay was thinking about how his basketball uniform had been in the heap of dirty clothes on the floor of his closet, in the bedroom that didn't exist anymore.

"Listen, Jay. I made a phone call this morning." The tone in Willis' voice was cautious, like he was about to say something he didn't quite believe was true. "And, ah ... well I talked to the coach over at Centreville. Good guy. Burke. Played with Acadia the year they won the Nationals. Knows his stuff. So anyway, we thought it would be a good idea if you signed up with him and his guys over there. Play out the rest of the season."

Jay could hardly believe his ears. What was it with everyone and their stupid, stupid, stupid ideas? "Come on, Allie," he said, not even looking at Coach Willis. "Let's get the hell out of here."

"You've got a class to go to, Allison," said the principal as she came out of her office beside Jay's mother. "Hurry along, please."

Allie squeezed Jay's hand and then slipped away. He was left standing there with three adults who had already signed, sealed, and delivered him into the hands of Richmond's main opponent, Centreville. Well, maybe they could make him go there, but they couldn't make him like it, and they couldn't make him play basketball. He would turn himself into a cardboard cutout and barely exist until things got back to normal.

4

Counter-Clockwise

The Todds came back, of course, after only one day in the Dominican Republic. Everything they said was an apology. Mr. Todd was most apologetic of all because he had been the one who had cleaned out their wood stove that Saturday afternoon, sure that the ashes he had shoveled into the wooden box were hardly even warm. He had placed the palm of his hand down on them, in fact. In the garage, he thought, they'd be absolutely cold in no time at all.

Sam fit into Centreville's primary class, hardly noticing the change. His new teacher's name was Mrs. Swinamer and when he talked to Jay at recess he kept mumbling, "Mrs. Swimminger, Mrs. Swimminger."

The basketball coach tried to treat Jay like he was already playing on the Cougars team. "Willis didn't have to tell me I was getting a top guy. I've seen you do your stuff. Great ball control. Great scoring. We're glad to have you aboard, Jay." He said to call him Burke — not Coach Burke, not Mr. Burke, not even Coach.

"I'm not playing basketball. Not here."

"Oh, I know it'll be odd. Anyone would feel that way at first. But trades happen in professional sports all the time, right? Think of this like you've been traded, except you won't be getting the big bucks like the pros do. Ha."

Jay didn't laugh.

He knew right away it was the coach's idea when Murphy came up to him at lunchtime in the school cafeteria. "How's it goin'?"

"It's not," replied Jay bluntly.

"Tough break about your house burning down."

"It didn't technically burn down." It was weird being right next to Murphy without a basketball in sight. Strangely, without the red and yellow uniform, he looked just like any other guy.

"Some of us are going to shoot a few baskets. Wanna come?"

"Not really."

"It's not the team or anything."

"Think I'll just stay here."

"I dunno. I'd have to play basketball no matter what."

"Even if you had to play for Richmond?"

"Basketball's basketball to me." Murphy got up. "We'll be in the gym if you change your mind."

"Yeah," said Jay.

When the bell rang at the end of that day, he climbed on the bus, took a seat right at the front where no one really wanted to sit. Sam was sitting a few seats behind him, already friends with another little guy from his class. Jay tried not to think about basketball, about Allie, about Colin, about Coach Willis, and about the next game Centreville would be playing against Richmond Academy.

* * *

It was Wednesday, four days since the fire. What was getting to Jay was that his parents were dealing with all kinds of things — insurance, phone calls to explain, phone calls to enquire, buying new clothes, rescuing a few things from the house, filling up boxes and putting them in storage, cleaning some family pictures that only had smoke damage and putting them in Gramp's living room, borrowing a bed for Sam and setting it up in the room with Jay. All those things were being dealt with, but no one was doing anything about how depressed Jay was because he had to go to Centreville School, and going to Centreville School meant no basketball.

The homework Jay had was all lame stuff he could do in minutes after supper or even in seconds just before he went to class. In social studies they were supposed to pick a topic to research. Jay picked the history of sneakers. Easy.

The guidance counsellor had phoned to say how wonderfully Sam was adjusting to Centreville and that Jay's academics were impressive. Burke called to say that you could encourage a guy all you want and get other players to strike up a conversation and all that, but when it came to the time when the whistle blew and the game started, you couldn't make a guy put on a uniform and play.

Jay's mom and dad had agreed that he could go to a movie with Allie even though it was a school night. They were probably feeling guilty about how everything was so messed up.

While he waited for his mom or dad to get home and drive him over to Richmond, he stayed in his room. He could hear Gramp and Sam and Rudy down in the kitchen having an afternoon snack together. Gramp laughed when Rudy howled for another piece of cookie and Sam kept saying "chicklet chop cookies" instead of chocolate chip. It was driving Jay nuts.

How could things change so drastically — flipside, 180 degrees, counter-clockwise?

* * *

At the mall, Jay waited for Allie outside the theatre. He also checked to make sure he had the twenty bucks in his wallet. Then he put his hand in front of his mouth and checked his breath. He dug a stick of gum out of his pocket anyway.

Allie came through the door at 6:15, just like they had planned. But, walking beside Allie was her best friend, Gina. Not like they had planned.

"Hi, Jay. Gina's coming too, okay?"

"Sure." What else was he supposed to say? He looked at Gina's thick and curly red hair, the small pattern of freckles that stained her cheeks, her large blue eyes that always read minds, and the pink bubble that was growing larger and larger and larger in front of her mouth. It burst.

"Which movie should we see?" He asked the question to no one in particular.

"Doesn't matter," said Allie and Gina at the same time.

They settled, finally, into their seats, balancing pop and popcorn while they removed their heavy jackets, scarves, and mitts. Jay was looking around at how empty the theatre was compared to how full the end of their row seemed to be.

He could smell Allie's shampoo — like strawberry or maybe raspberry. When she had arrived at the mall, her long brown hair had been tied in a ponytail that stuck out through the back loop of her blue ball cap. Now she took the cap off, letting her hair fall in a shiny river to her shoulders, like an ad on TV. She turned and smiled at him, as if she knew he was thinking about that ad. Her teeth were an ad too. And her green eyes might have been from a magazine, especially since she was wearing her new tinted contact lenses.

Before he had a chance to give her a TV smile back, Allie turned suddenly to Gina.

He couldn't hear what Gina was saying but he heard Allie

ask, "Where? Who with?" Both their heads swivelled around like searchlights on a dark sea.

"Who you guys looking for?"

"No one."

"That should make things easy," he said sarcastically. He hated coming out with that remark. But Allie laughed, so she must've only caught the words, not the sarcastic tone. Lucky.

His popcorn was almost gone before the previews were over and the feature presentation started. His hands felt greasy. Glancing sideways at Allie who was concentrating on the screen, he dipped his fingers into the pop and fluttered them quietly, one hand, then the other. He stuffed his fingers into a pile of napkins and dried them off. There.

He moved his elbow on the armrest so his arm was touching Allie's. He put his hand over hers and squeezed. She curled her fingers into his fingers and squeezed back. They watched about a half hour of the movie that way.

Then, he let go of her hand and put his arm across the back of her seat. His fingers momentarily got caught in Gina's wild curls and she turned around, startled, as if some stranger had grabbed her hair.

"Sorry," he said, leaning forward.

"What?" said Allie.

"I accidentally grabbed Gina's hair."

Gina was smoothing the red mass, as if that would do anything to control it.

Jay tried again. This time, he bent his elbow and placed it just behind his own seat. His hand was now on Allie's shoulder closest to him and he could feel her collarbone through her T-shirt.

They watched another half hour of the movie.

The guy in bed on the screen was touching the long black hair of the woman who was sitting on the side of the bed. She wasn't sure about that guy or about the bed. She had no clothes on, but all you could see were bare shoulders. Jay was thinking about how, in movies that weren't rated R, the female actors probably had on tube tops and jeans when they did these sexy scenes where only their bare shoulders were showing.

Then the guy in the bed lifted a long strand of the woman's black hair and tucked it gently behind her ear. That's when Jay thought of it: the earlobe move.

He straightened up a bit and moved his elbow back far enough so his fingers were right under Allie's ear. His mom had rubbed his dad's earlobe, using her thumb and first finger. The way Jay was sitting, he was going to have to make it a backhand kind of move. No problem.

He waited until the guy in bed turned out the lights and the woman lay down beside him. Jay was still thinking about her tube top and jeans. The music went soft. Jay twisted his wrist slightly and tugged on Allie's earlobe.

"Ow!"

"Oh geez. Sorry. I didn't—"

"What?" Gina was saying, leaning forward.

"Jay pinched my ear."

"I didn't mean to. It was …" The earlobe move. Jay brought his arm back down and returned it to the safety of the armrest. He took a sip of his pop. It tasted like salt and butter.

They watched the last half hour of the movie. Jay wasn't exactly disappointed in the whole date so far, but, when all the facts were totalled up, he wasn't thrilled either.

With only minutes left in the movie, Allie leaned against his arm and put her head on his shoulder. He took her hand. She moved her other hand up to the side of his chin and turned his face directly into hers. That's how the movie ended. Kisses and more kisses. Who cared about Gina? Who cared about what happened to the guy and that woman with black hair and tube top and jeans?

* * *

Sam was sleeping in a tangle of bedclothes when Jay tiptoed into the bedroom. Without turning on the light, he stripped down to his boxers and crawled into bed. Before he had much chance to rewind the whole kissing scene and press play, Jay was fast asleep too.

* * *

The basketball court was liquid shiny and as large as a football field. A player loped down the outside lane, bouncing a basketball the colour of a bright pumpkin. With each contact of the ball and the floor, the circular shape would melt like a huge orange raindrop into the liquid floor. Then up it would come again out of the water, reshaping into a circle before it made contact with the player's large palm. Down again. Melt. Up again. Circle.

Jay's eyes followed the player in the same way a TV camera would, keeping up with him, showing all the details of his moves. His arms were long and his right shoulder rippled with the motion of bouncing the basketball. His hand spread across the top of the ball like a giant's. The player, wearing the red and yellow Cougar colours, turned to face Jay. It was Mike Murphy, as tall as a tree and moving without any effort, without any speed, and without any noise. Mike smiled at Jay and passed the ball in a straight, slow line right into his hands.

The pumpkin orange melted through Jay's fingers, then swirled up into a solid circle again. Jay held the ball, unguarded in this silent basketball game. Why had Mike passed the ball to him?

Murphy loped along to the far end of the long shiny court. He turned and raised his hands to accept the pass.

Jay pushed the basketball in what he thought would be a quick snap pass. Why was he passing the ball to a Centreville player? It drifted slowly, uninterrupted, into Mike's hands. There it melted, reformed into the orange circle, then spun up and away from Mike's fingertips, in through the hoop.

Two points! Victory! Championship!

Players swarmed Mike and Jay. Fans flooded onto the court from the bleachers.

Allie was there in front of Jay, now. She kissed him. Soft, warm, strawberry kisses. He folded his arms around her and pulled her close. That's when he noticed the colours of the basketball jersey he was wearing.

Red and yellow. Centreville Cougar's colours.

5

Caution

It was dark when Jay's father got home from work at six o'clock on Friday. As if things weren't depressing enough, these winter days shut down for the night when the afternoon was barely over. A light snow was falling.

Jay was heading to Colin's house to stay overnight. He tossed his backpack into the van and belted himself into the passenger seat.

"Got everything you need?"

"Yeah."

"What about money?"

"Mom gave me some."

Short answers to questions gave the hint that Jay didn't actually want to talk. His father took the hint. There was a down side to this silence. He knew his father was thinking, but Jay couldn't guess exactly what he was thinking about. Maybe he was just tired of driving from Richmond to Centreville and, like now, driving back to Richmond again. Maybe he understood how depressing it was for Jay to be switching schools and not playing basketball. Maybe he was trying to figure out how to change the situation.

They drove along the old highway. Not much of anything was visible except small snowflakes spiralling out of the darkness toward the windshield. It was like being in a spaceship moving forward through thousands of stars. A salt truck must have just gone along the same route because snow was accumulating on the trees, fields, roofs, and mailboxes but not on the narrow highway in front of them.

"You going to take a look at the house?" asked Mr. Hirtle.

"Huh?" The question caught Jay off guard, even though the house was on his mind a lot. Pictures would just pop into his head, like now, when he suddenly imagined the way his old bedroom would be filling up with snow right this very minute.

"I was over there today," said his father. "I go every day. Can't stop myself. Can't actually believe it, I guess."

"Me neither."

"It takes the best right out of you." They passed a sign: *Richmond 3 km.* "If you want, we could go together. Right now. Might be better if I'm there with you."

"Colin's waiting for me. Besides, it's too dark to see anything." Jay could feel a kind of thickness in his throat, as if he'd swallowed something that didn't go all the way down. Something dry and tasteless.

"Right. Sure."

They turned into the circular driveway. Colin's family home was three storeys high and painted red, just as it had been 120 years ago when it was first built. A wide veranda went all the way across the front and down one side.

"If you decide to go see the house tomorrow with Colin, well, you'll have to be ready. It won't be what you expect."

The car skidded just a bit in the slick layer of snow that covered the driveway.

"Make sure you're over at the hospital when Mom gets off at four tomorrow."

"Right." Jay hauled his backpack out of the van. Although

he said thanks, the word was muffled by the thud of the door as he slid it shut. He walked up the steps to the veranda, knowing his father was still watching him. Jay wished he could turn around and say something, like, "see ya" or "I appreciate that you drove me all the way back over here again," or "the fire wasn't your fault." He rang the doorbell and the melody of the chimes sounded in the front hall.

When Colin answered the door, Jay could hear the van slowly move out of the driveway.

"Geez. I didn't know it was snowing."

"It's not much. Couple of centimeters," said Jay.

"We ordered pizza. The works, no onions."

"Hello, Jay," said Colin's mother. "How's your family? I can't believe what you have gone through. And the way the fire started. What was he thinking?"

"We're okay. Thanks." Jay didn't really want to say much. It was like everyone was staring in through a wide-open window at everything his family was doing.

"Well, I'm glad you've come to stay the night with Colin. I'm sure he's been missing you all week."

Their grey cat curled around Jay's ankles. "Hi, Smudge," he said, tickling the cat's ears.

"When the pizza gets here, I'll give you boys a shout. Dad's down in the rec room with Shauna playing ping-pong — I mean table tennis. Shauna says ping-pong is out these days."

"Thanks, Mrs. Hebb."

"Bring your stuff," said Colin, already halfway up the wide staircase.

Jay dumped his backpack on the floor and Colin shuffled through the CDs. The first cut blasted out. Colin played air guitar and sang along, his eyes squeezed shut.

"I think I should be able to play in the tournament over at

MacLeod next weekend," said Jay before another song filled the room. "I'm hatin' this. It's like I'm kicked off the team."

"Real bummer."

"So I'm forced to be over at Centreville for a couple months. So what? It's not like I'm permanent there. Think I'll get Dad to call Coach Willis."

"Worth a try."

"I don't have my uniform anymore. It was in my closet."

"There's other uniforms."

"Anyone say anything? About how I'm not at school or at practice?"

"Sure. Coach talked about the fire and about us being there for one of our guys. We're sending a basket of stuff tomorrow. Fruit and chocolate and stuff like that. Not like it's a surprise."

But Jay was surprised. Baskets were for people in hospitals or someone who broke a leg. It bugged him that the team was thinking of his family like they had something wrong with them.

Later, when all the lights in the house were out and the silent snow was still falling, Jay lay awake in a sleeping bag on the air mattress next to Colin's bed. He was thinking about how someone else's sleeping bag wasn't like your own. It had unfamiliar musty smells. The zipper stuck in a place you weren't use to. He thought about how you missed all the normal things that you didn't even think about when you used to have your own sleeping bag.

The rumble of a snowplow along the narrow street woke Jay out of a deep sleep. Colin's bed was empty. Jay crawled out of the sleeping bag and hauled on his jeans and sweater. The clock on the bedside table read 10:53.

"Grab a shower if you want," said Colin, coming into the room and throwing his wet towel across a chair. "Mom's making pancakes." He put on his jeans and a black sweatshirt, then dug into a drawer for socks. "What'll we do after we eat?"

"I dunno. Might call Allie. Maybe she'll meet us over at the mall."

"Gina'll be there. She's always with Allie, like they're attached at the brain or something. It bugs me."

Jay was letting the air out of the mattress, rolling it and pressing down with both hands. "Why should you be bugged? Unless you've got something goin' with Gina."

"Get real."

Jay gave a little chuckle.

"What's that supposed to mean?"

"What?"

"Laughing like that."

"Like what?"

"Oh, forget it." Colin gave Jay a look that said stop wasting my time. "I'll save you a couple pancakes." He left the bedroom and went downstairs.

Jay picked up the bedside phone and dialed Allie's number.

"Hi, Colin." There was her voice, still sexy, still turquoise.

"It's me. Jay."

"Oh. I thought it was Colin. His number's on the display."

"I'm at his place. I told you I was coming over here, remember?"

"Yeah. Right. Forgot."

Their conversation was short. Too short. No, she wasn't going to be able to meet him and Colin at the mall because she and Gina had to work on a health project all afternoon. It was due on Monday. She'd call him tomorrow night.

Jay felt weird. Something in Allie's voice was different. For sure she didn't sound like the same girl he had been kissing at the movie two nights ago. What was with her anyway?

The sun was shining but it didn't have a chance against the freezing temperatures. Nothing was melting. As Jay and Colin walked along the sidewalk towards the mall, their sneakers made sharp squeaking sounds against the snow where people hadn't shovelled. Jay pulled the black toque down over his ears and switched his backpack from one shoulder to the other.

"Something's weird with Allie."

"Weird how?"

"Just weird. No way she has to work all day on a stupid health project. It's like … I dunno."

"How about if we go over to your house?" said Colin. "Take a look. I was there Monday. You should see the place. It's unreal."

"Ah, sure. Okay." But Jay was thinking it wasn't going to be okay at all.

Sheets of ice spilled along the street and encrusted the rubble that had once been the Todds' garage. Part of the garage roof lay on its back in the rubble with a few scorched rows of yellow vinyl siding and a small window that wasn't even broken. A pair of grass clippers and a rake lay where the side door used to be. Blackened branches of a large bush stuck out through the new layer of snow.

From the front, the Hirtles' house didn't look too damaged at all. One upstairs window was smashed, probably by a fire-fighter. Down the side of the house, Jay could see the smudge from smoke all along the white eaves. The garage and the house were cordoned off with yellow plastic ribbon: CAUTION. FIRE LINE. DO NOT CROSS. The yellow ribbon was secured to a large garbage can near what used to be the Todds' garage and to a metal pole that used to be a driveway light. Then it went across the front lawn and all the way around the back of the Hirtles' house. CAUTION. FIRE LINE. DO NOT CROSS.

Jay's heart was thumping, just like it had a week ago when the fire was consuming the garage and threatening to explode any gas tanks inside.

"Stinks," said Colin.

Jay pictured his father standing right where he was now. Coming every day and looking at the mess. Even the new layer of snow couldn't hide the destruction. Large garage beams were reduced to charred wood, rippled with shiny charcoal and splintered where they broke. The whole scene was impossible.

"You should see the back. It's like a bomb hit there. I mean it."

"It says not to cross."

"That doesn't mean if it's your house." Colin ducked under the caution tape.

"Let's get goin'. I'm freezin'." Just as he turned to leave, Jay caught a glimpse of Mrs. Todd at her living room window, holding back the curtains enough to see out. She was another reason to get out of there fast. He sure didn't want to have to listen to her apologizing and asking questions and practically having a nervous breakdown.

"What's the big deal? It's not like the whole house got burned."

It's not like your house got burnt either. And it's not like your bedroom disappeared. And it's not like what's left of all your stuff stinks like a garbage fire.

Inside the mall, Jay hauled off his toque and stuffed it into his jacket pocket. Another Saturday at the mall. Same old thing: people everywhere, some shopping and some just hanging out; sun shining down through the large skylights; winter sales, 70 per cent off.

They walked around a bit, then talked to a few people they knew from school. Everyone was telling Jay they were sorry about his house and about how he wasn't at Richmond Academy now. Nothing they said made him feel any better. The more people said they were sorry, the more depressed he got.

"What time is it?" he asked Colin.

"Two-thirty. When're you meeting your mom?"

"Four."

"What'll we do now?"

"I dunno. Let's just go somewhere."

As they cut across the parking lot of the mall, someone shouted, "Hey, Jay! Jay! Over here!" From the passenger side of a parked truck, Murphy was waving out the window.

"I can't believe it," scowled Colin. "Murphy. Waving like a maniac."

"Hi," said Jay without much enthusiasm.

Colin turned and walked away.

"What's with him?" said Murphy.

Jay glanced over his shoulder but Colin wasn't looking back. "Nothin's wrong. He's just—"

"He's got an attitude, if you ask me. Last week when I was here, he came over and started mouthing off. Called me a hick."

"I know. I mean, I know he says stuff like that."

"A loser." Then Murphy tried to change the subject. "So how's it goin' anyway?"

"Not bad." *Not good.* "Listen, I gotta go catch up with him."

"Yeah. Well, see you in school, then."

"Right."

Jay caught up with Colin, feeling pretty well tired of the whole day: the phone call to Allie, his burned house with all that yellow caution tape, and now Colin acting weird again.

But it got worse.

"Looks like you're making friends with the enemy."

"Cut it out."

"I'm just saying what it looks like."

"The guy just said hi."

"Same guy who slammed you in the head and just about left you in a coma. Maybe you lost your memory or something."

"Look," said Jay, stopping and shifting his backpack to his other shoulder, "I gotta go meet Mom."

"Right." Colin was still walking, his hands stuffed into his pockets and his shoulders hunched to his ears.

There was almost a whole hour before his mother would get off work, but Jay was thinking that sitting in the emergency waiting room reading magazines from a hundred years ago would be a lot better than walking around in the freezing cold with a guy who wasn't even acting like a friend anymore.

"I'll give you a call tomorrow maybe. Thanks for the pizza and everything."

"Sure. I'll see ya, then."

* * *

When Jay and his mother got to Gramp's, there was the gift basket on the coffee table. "To Jay and his family from Richmond Academy Junior Boys Basketball Team." Sam was consuming a small box of raisins and Gramp was eating a banana. Rudy was sitting in front of them, drooling.

"Oh, how thoughtful," said Jay's mom.

"It came about an hour ago," said his father. "Apples, grapes, raisins. Even some chocolates. Everything but the kitchen sink. And we could've used a kitchen sink."

They all laughed except Jay. He didn't even want to look at the stuff in that basket. He lugged his backpack upstairs, trying to ignore Sam's singsong voice repeating "sitchen kink."

Because there was nothing better to do, Jay dug out the

printed pages from his web search on the history of sneakers and started to highlight facts he might use in his social studies project.

In the third period of the hockey game on TV, when everyone else was in bed, Jay told his father that he and Colin had gone over to their house that afternoon.

"How'd that go?"

"It was weird."

"Hard to believe, for sure."

"All that yellow caution stuff. Like a crime scene or something. Colin wanted to go around back. He went there on Monday he said. But I didn't go."

"Why?"

"It felt creepy."

"Tell you what. Tomorrow we'll all go over there. It'd be good for the whole family to take a look together. Maybe give us a chance to think about how we'll renovate."

"Sure. Okay. May as well try to get used to it, I guess."

"That's what I've been saying to myself all week."

6

Disappearing

On Sunday afternoon, they drove over to Richmond. Rudy started whining about two blocks away from the house and Jay's mother had to calm him down by saying, "It's okay, Rudy. It's okay." It seemed as if she was trying to convince the whole family that things would be okay.

As they turned onto their street, Gramp said, "It's only a house. What's important is what's right here inside this car."

Sam held his mother's hand and Rudy stuck close by, sniffing the cold wind that carried traces of charred wood. Jay knew this wasn't easy for Sam because, for once, he wasn't talking. Probably he was squeezing his mother's fingers tightly.

Mrs. Todd came out of her house and Mr. Todd was right behind her. Their eyes were almost melting with sadness. "I want all of you to come over for tea," said Mrs. Todd. "After…. When you're ready." Then they both went back in, out of the cold and away from watching the Hirtle family face the destruction.

Jay could hear his mother's voice softly cooing to Sam. Although he couldn't hear her words, they were soothing him a bit too. Everyone went past the yellow caution ribbon. They walked along the snow-covered driveway to the back of the house.

Jay's stomach ached sharply. His throat was dry and tight.

Nothing was real and everything was real. The back porch was gone, and only half of the kitchen was still there. The fridge looked ridiculous now, scorched and exposed to the outdoors. On top of the snowdrift beneath Jay's bedroom lay his mattress, scorched in places and burned through to the coils in other places. His mostly burned quilt was partly covered by the new snow. Jay thought about crawling into bed on cold nights, pulling the quilt up over his ears, finding that spot in the mattress where his body settled in.

"Well, well, well," said Gramp. "My oh my oh my."

Jay's mother turned to walk back up the driveway with Sam. "Brian, let's go home to Gramp's. I'll tell Mrs. Todd we'll have tea another time."

"Good idea."

Sam called Rudy. Gramp followed behind the dog.

Jay didn't move.

"You okay?" His father put his hand on Jay's back.

"No," said Jay. The way he felt, his face must look as white as all that new snow.

"No," repeated his father. Then he gave him a strong hug, holding on tightly even when Jay started to pull away.

* * *

The next evening the architect came to Gramp's house. Everyone had something to add to the wish list: a window seat in the kitchen; cupboards with stained-glass doors; a large deck out back; a closet in Jay's room big enough to walk in and a bed built against the wall like a ship's captain's bed with two large drawers underneath. Sam's bedroom, although not at all damaged by the fire, would have the same captain's bed and the same large closet.

"Before the end of May," said the architect, "you'll have your dream home and that fire will be in your historical past."

"If she says the end of May, then I say it'll be the end of July," said Jay's father, after they had waved goodbye to the architect and closed the front door behind her.

Jay knew one thing for certain: he wasn't going to ask his father to make any phone calls to help him play basketball for Richmond Academy. After all the family had gone through, was still going through, he couldn't ask his father to solve this basketball problem. He'd have to do it himself, even though he was feeling so weird. So confused.

Besides all that, there was another problem he couldn't exactly figure out. What was with Allie? She had called him up last night like she said she would. She talked about that health project and about some kind of stupid ribbon Gina was going to put through the loose-leaf holes to hold the thing together. In other words, she talked about nothing. He didn't mention that his whole family had gone together to see the damage done by the fire. He didn't tell her that Colin was starting to act like a stick of dynamite at the end of a slow fuse. And he didn't bother to tell her that he was going to try somehow to play for Richmond at the weekend tournament.

Silence gave him more time to think.

He hadn't phoned Colin since Saturday. Things were depressing enough without hearing Colin rave on about how Murphy was a maniac or about how Jay was making friends with the enemy.

* * *

On Wednesday, Jay finally got up the nerve to see the principal of Centreville about how he wanted to keep playing basketball for Richmond. His plan was to start by convincing Mr. Roden-hizer that it was a good idea. Then the Centreville principal would make a phone call to the principal at Richmond while Jay was still there in the office, and the deal would be done.

He had gone over in his mind what he intended to say, but all that rehearsing had been a waste of time. Jay wasn't in the office two seconds when Mr. Rodenhizer got on a tangent of blah blah blah ... here in your father's old school ... blah blah blah ... proud to have you aboard.

Then he got up from behind his shiny expansive desk and said, "Son, there's something I want you to see. It's in the hall outside the library. Come along."

Jay followed as he was told.

"Now, look there," said Mr. Rodenhizer. "Ever see that?"

It was the picture of the Centreville basketball team with his father standing in the middle row, holding one end of the championship flag.

"Yes," said Jay. "In Dad's yearbook."

"Regionals in 1989. Centreville has only lost the Regionals a half-dozen times in forty-six years of play. Not a bad record, hey?"

"No, sir." *That record'll be blown out of the water by Richmond.*

"Now you have the opportunity to wear the red and yellow uniform, just like your father."

I'll be in white and blue.

"Burke tells me he's got a spot on the team waiting for you. You'll fit right in."

Wrong.

"I'm glad you came to see me today, Jay. Everyone's been worried, of course, and we can see you're not totally happy with the move here. But you're a young man now. Your family's been through a terrible crisis and they've got to build back up. This is how you can help. I'm telling you, it'll make a big difference. Once you're on the team, a lot of this negativity will be behind you. You'll move your life forward. You'll see the silver lining in those dark clouds."

Jay was thinking that Mr. Rodenhizer had read too many sympathy cards or else those chicken soup books.

"I'll tell Mr. Burke to have your uniform ready before you go home today."

With ten minutes still remaining before the noon break ended, Jay walked directly to Mr. Burke's office.

"Sir, I gotta say something to you about playing basketball for Centreville."

"Come on in. Sit down."

"I don't need to sit down, sir."

"Burke, remember? Just Burke."

"Yeah, well, all I need is to tell you I haven't changed my mind. I won't be playing for Centreville."

"Got your uniform right here." He held out the carefully folded shorts and jersey. "You take a bit of time to think things over."

"I already did the thinking, sir. Burke. But I appreciate that you made a spot for me on your team. I mean it. So anyway, well, I'll see ya."

Now Jay had to prepare himself for the weekend tournament. It was going to be a whole new game this time because he'd be taking in the action from the bleachers.

* * *

On Friday evening, Jay's mother dropped him off at Dr. A. C. MacLeod School. He could watch the early game between

Richmond Academy and MacLeod in the time it was going to take her go to over to Richmond to check on a few patients, get the groceries, and then drive back to pick him up.

"Are you meeting Allie?" his mother asked.

"Maybe. I'm not sure." Jay hadn't bothered to phone anyone to tell them he was going to the tournament. And no one had phoned him either.

"Jay, I know this isn't easy. I'm proud of you, really. Coming here to watch your team. Showing your support, even when you can't play."

"I can play."

"I know you can play." She looked at the people getting out of vehicles and heading towards the school entrance. "I don't know how to change what's happened. We're struggling. Your father and I need you to understand."

"I understand. And I'm not asking for anything anymore. I even picked out the kind of closet and bed and stuff for my room, like you guys wanted me to."

"Didn't you want those things?"

"I want to play basketball."

"You could play for Centreville. Mr. Burke told us he had a uniform for you and everything."

"Mom, I'm not changing my mind about that. I told him and I told Mr. Rodenhizer. No one's got ears anymore."

"We just want you to be happy, Jay. We know how important basketball was to you, but—"

"Is."

She squeezed his hand as if she knew what he was thinking. But she didn't.

"I better get in there," he said.

The gymnasium was filling up with parents, brothers and sisters, and fans, mostly from MacLeod. The Centreville play-

ers were in the bleachers, not yet dressed for the game they
would play next against Lakeview. If Mr. Burke or Murphy or
anyone else from Centreville saw him, Jay didn't know because
he didn't spend any time looking over there. He avoided the few
Richmond fans who had bothered to show up. Gina's red hair
wasn't in sight, so Allie couldn't be around either.

He stepped up into the middle of the bleachers and disappeared among the MacLeod fans.

When the Richmond and MacLeod players jogged onto the
court, people all around him jumped up, cheering and clapping.
Jay watched his old team go through their warm-up: stretches,
two laps around the gym, and then into a three-man weave drill.

He felt awful.

When Coach Willis called his team over to the bench in a
huddle, Jay knew he'd be saying stuff like *Pick your man and
stay with him*; or *If your eyes aren't on that basketball, they're
on the wrong thing*; or *I want a win from start to finish, boys*.

Colin walked to the middle of the basketball court and
shook hands with MacLeod's centre. He had taken over Jay's
job of starting centre. The referee tossed the ball up into the air
and blew the whistle, beginning the Fourth Annual Dr. A. C.
MacLeod Invitational Basketball Tournament.

Jay could barely breathe, squashed in between two MacLeod
fans who kept jumping up and then landing even closer to his
small square of space on the bleacher. Despite the bullet-fast
action of the game and the fact that Richmond held on to the lead,
he continued to feel awful. His stomach seemed as if it was
stuffed with marshmallows, sweet and sticky.

Coach Willis must have called for a 3–2 zone in front of the
MacLeod basket. There was Tyler playing point guard, Jay's old
position in that defense play. When the right wing grabbed the
rebound and threw the ball to Tyler, Jay's legs twitched and his

feet lifted off the bleacher as though it was his responsibility to lose the guard and get the ball down the outside lane.

This was the first time he'd ever watched his team play, not counting practice or watching from the bench until it was his turn to get back into the game. It was weird. Sure, he knew all those guys, and sure he knew the plays they were making. But it was like they were aliens playing basketball on another planet.

As the game continued, the sweet sticky sensation in his stomach got worse. Richmond was doing okay without him. By half time, Tyler and Brendon, with 10 points each, were tied for the honour of Richmond high scorer. At least they hadn't topped Jay's half-time best of 14.

Colin kept controlling most of the action under the basket. It was more than his height; it was his fierce concentration. Once he did a perfect give and go, scoring an easy two points in a lay-up that left MacLeod's defense staring up at the bottom of his sneakers.

Now, a MacLeod player was pressing down the inside lane, bouncing the ball out of Colin's reach. Colin sped up and then planted himself firmly in his opponent's path for what should have been a close-out. The MacLeod guy put his left elbow out and crossed over in front of Colin without missing a beat. As Colin scrambled to catch up, the MacLeod player made a quick pass to his post who somehow was alone at the elbow of the key. The ball was up and in.

Almost everyone was looking at the ball swish through the hoop and the way the net leaped when the points were scored. But Jay was looking at Colin. What he saw surprised him. Colin pretended to be scratching the corner of his eye as he walked past his MacLeod opponent. He made a smooth turn, not even looking at the guy, and nudged him with his elbow. He kept on walking like nothing had happened. The MacLeod guy looked confused, not sure whether the bump had been intentional.

Jay wondered if this was the kind of stuff Colin did all the time, like it was part of his game and no one else knew it. It was such a natural and sly move, threatening without being obvious.

He checked the MacLeod fans on either side of him. They weren't taking any notice of the nudge. Colin had got away with it.

As play continued, Jay found himself more interested in looking around the bleachers than at the action on the court. He could tell which guys were on teams waiting for their turn in the tournament, even though they weren't wearing their uniforms yet. It was the way they put their elbows on their knees or leaned over to say something about a play or didn't really get excited about fumbles or points. If anyone had been looking at Jay sitting there, they'd be able to tell that he wasn't on any team. He was practically invisible.

Eventually, he didn't even care who won the game. How could he care? You had to be a basketball player or a fan if you were going to care. Jay wasn't a basketball player anymore, and he wasn't really a fan now either.

Before the game ended, he managed to slip out of the gym without being noticed by anyone from Richmond or from Centreville. There was no way he was going to come back to watch any more tournament games. What was the point?

While he waited for his mother inside the school's front entrance, leaning on the large metal door handles and looking out into the darkened parking lot, Jay tried to give himself a pep talk about getting off the bleachers and back into basketball. Somehow. Before it was too late.

7

Hitchhiking to Nowhere

Sam and Jay both heard the bus rumbling along the road in front of Gramp's house. It would make one stop over by Whynot's General Store, then turn around and pick them up. They had seven minutes to bolt down breakfast, grab their stuff, and start down the lane.

This was the beginning of week number three at Centreville School.

Sam seemed to be coping pretty well with things now. After they had gone to look at their house, he hadn't quite been himself. He had slept downstairs with his parents a couple of times. Jay had heard his father carrying Sam back to his own bed after he had fallen asleep. One morning, Jay overheard his mom whispering to Sam. It probably had something to do with being a "big boy" and must have also involved a deal. Sam started looking at two-wheel bikes in the catalogues.

When they got off the bus, Sam and Jay walked into school together. Centreville was a single-storey building, stretched out in one long line with a large square section in the middle. The square included the front entrance, the gymnasium, and a small cafeteria. One end of the long line was the elementary wing and the other end was the junior-high wing.

"Check ya later, buddy," said Jay to Sam and watched him

saunter along, joining the other little kids. Some were sitting on
the floor hauling off boots and some were organizing scarves
and mittens on low hooks that were individually labelled with
each child's name.

The elementary wing was tidy, clean, and colourful. Classroom doors were decorated with cut outs of balloons or animals
and hundreds of Valentine hearts. Teachers were helping kids
with jammed zippers or listening to things they had to say.

Jay turned towards the junior-high wing. What a contrast!
The dreary halls were lined with lockers painted a sick green.
Nothing was on the doors of the classrooms except the names
of teachers in small black letters: J. James, G. Comeau, R. Himmelman — like their first names were some kind of big secret.
They were all probably in the staff room right now, complain-
ing about kids who failed tests and wishing they could haul out
cigarettes to go with their litres of coffee.

Even though it was only 8:46, there was already garbage on
the floor in the junior-high wing — a chip bag and the wrapper
from a cereal bar. The polished gleam on the tiled floor wouldn't
last past recess.

Jay walked towards his classroom, the second-last one on
the left. But when he got there, he kept right on walking out the
side door, across the field on a path beaten down through the
deep drifts of snow, and far enough along the highway to be out
of sight of the school.

He shifted his backpack to his left shoulder, stuck out his
right thumb, and started walking backwards towards Richmond.

His plan was to try to convince the principal of Richmond
Academy to get him back on the basketball team, since his attempt
with Centreville's principal had hit a brick wall. Again, Jay
rehearsed what he would say: *Why should I be punished just
because there was a fire at our house? What's the difference if I go*

to one school and play basketball for another? And besides, the move to Centreville is just temporary.

What he wouldn't say to the principal was that he felt like he was disappearing.

The snow that had fallen into his sneakers when he crossed the field behind Centreville School was now turning to ice as he plodded along the highway. The way cars were zooming past him, the drivers must be thinking Jay was some kind of criminal in training. If it was because of the way his black toque was pulled down over his ears, then too bad. In this iceberg cold, he wasn't going to take it off and risk frostbite, even if it might mean he'd get a drive faster. And if someone his parents knew stopped to give him a lift, he'd just have to deal with that problem later.

By the time he got to Richmond Academy, thanks to the guy in a bread truck, it was already recess. The front hallway was crowded with people standing in small clusters talking about nothing and looking around at everyone. The first people he saw were a couple of guys on his basketball team.

"Hey, Jay. What's up? How come you're over here?"

"Came to see Ms. Morrison. About maybe still playing on the team."

"Cool," said one of the guys.

"Coulda used you over at MacLeod this weekend. We got creamed."

"Who won the tournament?"

"Centreville." The two guys looked awkwardly at each other, like no one should be mentioning Centreville out loud.

Jay looked away. That's when he saw Gina's red hair at the far end of the crowded hallway. Allie must be close by. "Check you guys later," he said and left without waiting for a response.

Yes, he could see Allie now. And Colin, too. He slipped past some girls who had formed a roadblock, then elbowed his way along, keeping Gina, Allie, and Colin in view. For a few seconds he had an old feeling, comfortable and familiar, as he headed towards his best friend and his girlfriend and Gina. It could have been any other recess on any other day at Richmond Academy.

But it wasn't.

Jay was closer now and getting ready to say something like *Hey, what's up with you guys?* when he realized that something was different, out of place somehow.

He stopped.

There was Gina standing beside Allie as usual. Their heads were close together and whatever they were saying was just for the two of them to hear. Colin was on the other side of Allie, his back to Jay. He wasn't just standing there. He was holding Allie's hand.

What's goin' on? What's with you two? Since when? All those thoughts went through Jay's mind like flashes of lightning, but he couldn't say a thing out loud. He was stunned.

And, he was disappearing even more.

Once again, he found himself out on the highway, hitchhiking, this time the two kilometers into the town from Richmond Academy. He got a ride almost as soon as he stuck out his thumb.

"Something bothering you, son?" asked the old man driving the truck.

"Toothache," mumbled Jay.

"Better get that looked at."

"Mm."

He got out at an intersection near the mall and muttered a thank you to the old man as he pulled his backpack out of the truck.

Jay headed directly to their house — what was left of it. A large metal dumpster was in the driveway, filled with scorched wood, smashed doors and windows, and other stuff that just wasn't worth trying to save. His old mattress was right there on top.

Another dumpster blocked the Todds' driveway. All he could see in that one was a bit of yellow siding and tons of torched wood.

No one was around, not even at the back of the house where most of the work had been going on. Maybe everyone took off for some place warm to have a coffee or lunch.

Workers had stripped the kitchen and Jay's bedroom above it down to the bare frame of the house. They had smashed away the cement foundation where the old porch had been. Bright orange tarpaulin was nailed over empty windows, over the entrance to the downstairs hallway, and over what used to be the door to Jay's bedroom.

It would take a million years to make that house look like anything normal. Suddenly, he was filled with boiling hot anger. "This house stinks! This bloody place isn't even a house!"

He ran out of the backyard, stopping abruptly next to the rusting dumpster. He picked up two chunks of charred wood that had fallen out of it, then stepped into the deep snow at the front of the house. With all the force his anger gave him, Jay hurled both chunks through the living room windows, smashing them with violent explosions of glass.

He ran and ran and ran. His lungs stung in the freezing cold and his legs were shaking when he finally stopped. He put his hands on his knees and leaned over to catch his breath, leaving two charcoal handprints on his jeans. The tears on his cheeks might have been from the icy wind in his face.

* * *

Now it was three o'clock. Jay had spent the rest of the day doing nothing except keeping warm at the mall. Banners and window displays and signs about season's specials screamed out from every possible corner. Today they were screaming about Valentine's Day: cupids, red hearts, diamond displays. For your sweetheart. Now and forever. *Yeah, right*, thought Jay.

He was looking into a large glass display case at a small silver heart-shaped locket on a silver chain. If pictures were put inside that tiny heart, they'd have to be smaller than a dime. Even though he probably wouldn't have bought a locket for Allie, Jay was overcome with the feeling that now he never could do it, even if he wanted to. It was very depressing.

"Can I help you?" asked the clerk.

"Um, no. No. That's okay. Just looking."

"These hearts are our Valentine feature, $27.99. A special something for a special someone."

Jay turned away and didn't look back.

He felt so exhausted he could have slept on one of those wooden benches with the green garbage bins beside them. But in a town this small, someone would've woken him up, probably thinking he needed rescuing. And he did.

By four o'clock, he was standing inside the emergency entrance of the hospital close to the vent where hot air blasted out. He would wait there for his mother. Her new car was in the parking lot, so she was still working.

"Jay! This is a surprise! What're you doing over here?" His mother could read a face as easily as she could read a thermometer taken out of a patient's mouth. "What's wrong?"

He kept his face frozen in neutral. "Nothing. But, I didn't exactly go to school today. Well, I did but—"

"Come on. Let's go home."

"We can't go home. It's not there anymore."

They faced each other in the freezing cold of the hospital parking lot. He blinked so she couldn't see deep into his eyes and know what was really going on.

They didn't talk much on the drive from Richmond over to Centreville. Jay turned the radio to a volume that only left room for listening.

When she had parked the car in Gramp's lane and turned off the ignition, Jay's mom turned to him, placing her hand gently on his knee. "All of us are feeling confused. Lost, really. Every time I wake up I have to remember where I am. And I don't think that will change soon. We're just going to have to do our best until we can move back home. How can I help you, Jay? How can I make things better?"

Tears slipped out of the small pools that filled his eyes, and they just kept streaming.

"Oh, sweetie, it'll be okay. I promise, I promise. It'll be okay." When she reached to put her arms around him, her right hand left a small smudge of charcoal on the back of his jacket.

Jay dried his eyes with the tips of his fingers and blew his nose into the wrinkled piece of tissue his mother offered. "It'll take forever before we can move back home."

"We'll move by summertime. That's not forever, now is it?"

"Everything's changed."

"It just feels that way. But really a lot is exactly the same. We're all together and, look, even our address is the same." She picked up the stack of mail with an elastic band around it, and grinned. "Bills, magazines, flyers — all still showing up in our mailbox."

Jay blew his nose again.

"Let's go inside. I'm hungry. And if I'm hungry, you're ravenous."

Jay went upstairs right away, avoiding looking at anyone with his bloodshot eyes. In the bathroom, he splashed his face with a bit of cold water. When he stepped back out into the hall, he caught a piece of conversation between his mom and dad who were apparently alone in the living room.

"The Todds weren't home." That was his father's voice.

"But somebody must've seen someone or heard the sound of glass."

Jay's heart jumped. They were talking about the smashed windows.

"When the carpenters got back after lunch, they found a couple of chunks of burned wood inside on the living room floor," said his father.

"Burned wood?"

"Must've been taken out of the dumpster. And there were deep tracks where the guy must've stood to throw them."

The guy. They didn't know it was Jay. Still his heart pounded.

"The police are going to keep a closer lookout. And the neighbours too."

"I think it's best if we don't talk about this to the boys," said Jay's mother.

"Yeah, I guess you're right. It wouldn't help if they knew that a vandal was treating our house like it's abandoned."

Jay went into his bedroom and closed the door noiselessly. He sat down on his bed and put his face into his hands. Now he was a vandal.

When he moved his hands away from his face, he noticed two charcoal handprints on the knees of his jeans. One handprint was smudged. Then he looked at the palms of his hands and saw a few traces of charcoal still there. He immediately pictured throwing the charred wood, running away, then leaning his blackened hands against his knees as he stopped to catch his breath. When his mother had placed her hand on his knee, she would have touched the charcoal handprint.

In a panic, he quickly took off his jeans and put on a different pair. Then, with a black sock, he rubbed the stains off and threw the jeans into the laundry basket. He washed his face and hands thoroughly. Feeling like a criminal hiding evidence, he threw the stained towel into the laundry basket too.

At the dinner table, he stared at his plate of potatoes and carrots and chicken, eating slowly and saying nothing. Everyone around him chatted about the usual things: the food, the weather, and the progress on the house. No one asked him how his day was. No one asked him what was wrong. That was a sure sign his mom had told his dad and Gramp about the crying scene in the car. Sam had built-in radar. He would've picked up on the tension and decided to just go along with the idea of not bothering his brother.

All Jay could think about was the dumpster, the chunks of wood, the thunderous anger that had pounded in his head, and the glass shattering into hundreds of ragged pieces. He couldn't look at anyone around the dinner table, especially his mother. He was wondering why she hadn't noticed any black on the palm of her hand.

8

Changing Colours

The storm began slowly out of the quiet darkness. Small snowflakes slanted past the light at the end of Gramp's lane as Jay stood in the bedroom window looking out. Inside the house, all was quiet.

"Little snow, big snow," Gramp would have said if he were standing there watching too. It meant that if the flakes were small, lots of snow was predicted in the storm; if the flakes were large, then there wouldn't be much snow at all. Tonight the snow would pile up and the world would disappear beneath drifts of white.

Tomorrow, school would definitely be cancelled. But even that couldn't lift Jay out of his depression. All he could think about was that he wasn't a basketball player anymore. Instead, he had become a vandal.

Sam was soundly sleeping, lying on his back with one arm up over his head. No worries. No nightmares.

Jay turned from the window and crawled back into bed. He still couldn't sleep. Thoughts kept appearing in his head like previews of movies. Just bits and pieces, like the image of Gina's red hair close to Allie's head, and Colin holding Allie's hand. He saw one chunk of wood and then the other tumbling towards those living room windows. He saw the look of worry in his mother's eyes. When he replayed the conversation he had overheard between his parents that evening, he felt ashamed. He wished those small flakes of snow could softly land on his bed and accumulate until no one would see him anymore.

The blackness outside the window had turned to a deep blue when Jay woke up. It was almost dawn. For most of the night, he had filled his brain with facts and tried to put them into some kind of logical order. Lots of things had been going wrong. Somehow, he had to figure out how to make things go right.

Suddenly, as if his brain had put the last piece of the jigsaw puzzle together, he knew exactly what he was going to do. He threw back the covers, stepped onto the hooked mat beside his bed, and hauled on his clothes that lay in a heap on the floor.

Sam stirred and turned over, trying to open his sleepy eyes.

"Go back to sleep, Sam. No school."

That zapped Sam wide awake. He scrambled out of bed and went to the window, staring out at the way the snow had drifted against the vehicles in the lane, had almost buried the old wharf, and had stuck to one side of the fish shack like frosting on the side of a cake. "Santa Clause snow," he said.

Jay went downstairs. He could hear his parents' voices, quiet morning talk, through the door of the living room where they slept on the hide-a-bed. He knocked softly.

"Mom? Dad? It's me."

He went in and sat on the edge of the bed, feeling like such a little kid. Littler than Sam.

"What's up, Jay?" asked his father, leaning back against his pillow. His mother smoothed her hair out of her eyes.

"I have to tell you guys something."

When he finished all the details — about hitchhiking, about Colin and Allie, about the smashed windows — he wasn't feeling like such a little kid anymore. And he wasn't feeling like a vandal, either.

"You already knew, didn't you, Mom? Even if you weren't a doctor, you'd notice if you had dirty hands."

"What you did really doesn't matter, Jay. Your father and I have been going over and over ways we could help to make this move easy for you, but ... well, we thought ... hoped ... you'd do okay."

"If it takes a couple of smashed windows for you to make us see what we already should've realized," said his dad, "then that's a small price to pay."

"I feel so stupid."

"You're not stupid. Although what you did was a bit on the stupid side, I have to admit."

"I'm gonna pay for the windows. With my allowance. And I'll get a job too."

His parents looked at each other, then his mother spoke for both of them. "That's a deal. We'll price the new windows today."

"By the looks of all that white stuff out there, you could probably get a job from Gramp shovelling some of it away."

"Start with my car, please," said his mom. "I'm on call at 8:30. Clyde will be here to plow out the lane any minute now, then you can get to work."

"And I'm going to be playing basketball. For Centreville, I mean. Tomorrow, I'll get my uniform from Mr. Burke." Jay got up and started towards the kitchen. "We play Richmond on Thursday." He didn't turn around, but he knew his parents' jaws would've dropped wide open.

The radio announced for the twentieth time, "All schools are closed in Lunenburg County, Queens, Shelburne, Yarmouth, Digby, and Annapolis Valley." Jay made the next move in his morning decision. He went to the phone and dialed.

"Hi." There was Allie's voice, but today it wasn't sexy. The turquoise color had faded. She must be looking at Gramp's name on call display. She must be feeling guilty.

"Hi. It's me."

"Oh, hi. School's cancelled. Cool, hey."

He decided to save her the small talk and get right to the point. "I was over at Richmond yesterday. It was recess and I saw you and Colin. When you were holding hands." He didn't give her any time to react. "I'm not bugged about it. Not now. Well, I'm bugged that I didn't know. But—"

"Jay, I … I mean … well, me and Gina were just hanging out with Colin and … well, at first I thought he liked her … but then … well we just—"

"You coulda told me."

"I wanted to tell you, but you moved away and—"

"You had lots of chances to say something."

"You don't have to be sarcastic."

"I'm not sarcastic. I'm just talking."

"I still like you, Jay. Like a friend though."

"Thanks, Allie. I'll have to think about if I still like you like a friend. I'll let you know. Well, bye, then."

He carefully replaced the receiver, thought a minute, then picked it up again and dialed Colin's number.

"Ah, hi. That you, Jay?"

Call display again. "Yeah, it's me. I was just talking to Allie."

"Allie? Oh, yeah?"

"May as well come right out and say the same thing to you I said to her. I was over at Richmond yesterday and I saw you guys holding hands. Thing is, I got more stuff to worry about right now, but I won't say it didn't get to me. It did. I was bugged. Big time."

"Look, I … we—"

"I already know about the *we* stuff, Colin. What's with all that we stuff and you wouldn't even tell your best friend what was going on? I got a feeling you guys've been holding hands ever since I moved over here to Centreville. Matter of fact, I just remembered about when I phoned her from your place last Saturday and she answered with this sexy voice and everything. She thought it was you because of call display."

"I was going to say something, but she told me to wait until she had a chance to tell you. And anyway, what's the big deal? It's not like you have the same girlfriend your whole life."

"Better tell Allie about that. She might find it interesting. Anyway, I gotta go shovel snow. There's not much else to say."

"You don't have to act all weird."

"I'm not acting all weird. I'm just me. And I gotta go, like I said. So I'll see ya on Thursday." Before Colin had a chance to make the connection between Thursday and the basketball game between Centreville and Richmond Academy, Jay hung up the phone.

Sam immediately walked into the kitchen, already dressed in his blue snowsuit, boots, toque, scarf, and mittens. He was carrying a small red shovel. "You're not all weird," said Sam.

"You shouldn't eavesdrop, buddy. It'll make your ears drop off."

* * *

"Glad you'll be joining our boys," said Mr. Burke when Jay went to the coach's office. "And there's practice today. three-thirty to five-thirty."

"I'll be there."

"Can't say for sure you'll be on the court tomorrow against Richmond."

"Oh. Well, yeah. Right. I guess—"

"It's not because Richmond's your old school. Not at all. You're on our team now and that's where your loyalty is. But any new player would need some time to work out with the team. Get used to our plays."

"I'll do my best, sir. Burke."

"See you after school then."

Jay went to his locker and stuffed his red and yellow uniform inside. He tried not to think about wearing that uniform on the basketball court with Richmond's white and blue all around him. It was going to be too weird passing the basketball to a Cougar, maybe even to Mike Murphy. He was experiencing a hazy sensation that he already knew what that was going to be like.

While they waited for Burke to come into the gym and get practice started, Mike Murphy made sure the ball was thrown to Jay a couple of times so he could take some shots. Each ball swished through the hoop. The smooth feel of the gym floor under his sneakers, the hollow sound that echoed against the walls and high into the rafters when he bounced the ball, the alert energy he felt in his legs and down his arms to the tips of his fingers — all this was as natural to Jay as taking a breath.

When he was introduced to the rest of the team, he tried memorizing the names: Jacob, Russ, Vince, Alex, Greg, Chris, Rob, Mac (whose name was really Chris too). Burke told everyone to shake hands with their new teammate and they did. Most of them seemed okay with a Richmond guy playing for Centreville. Jay figured it was probably easier for the regional champs to relax when someone from another school joined their team. Or maybe Burke had somehow warned them, given them the "his loyalty is with us now" speech.

Burke blew the whistle and made a circle in the air with his raised arm. "Everyone do the loop ten times! Let's go!"

When they were barely finished jogging around the perimeter of the gym, he blew the whistle again. "Let's see some ball control. Everyone get a basketball and do three more laps."

The noise in the gym went up by ten decibels as twelve guys and twelve basketballs got to work.

"Okay!" yelled Burke. "Foul shots! Mike, take the first line down to the other basket. Vince, you lead the second line up here. Jay, you're behind Alex."

Burke studied every shot and gave an instant review: "Beauty. Sloppy. Beauty. Lucky. Sloppy. Lucky."

Jay's first foul shot got the review he wanted: Beauty.

They practised pick and roll, where Jay screened for Mike. When he turned away from Mike's defender in a smooth roll, he positioned himself under the basket in case Mike's shot missed the hoop.

Burke blew his whistle and shouted for the guys to put on pinnies, six players in black and six in green. They started with a man-to-man defense and Jay found himself on the ball right away. With his long arms outstretched and his feet placed firmly in front of the offensive player, he easily blocked him and forced a pass that was intercepted. When Rob dumped the two points through the hoop, Mike gave Jay a loud high five.

Basketball was once again bubbling in Jay's veins. Even though he was in Centreville's gym playing with the Cougars, it didn't feel strange at all. It felt like basketball, pure and simple. He was definitely off the bleachers and back in the game.

The two-hour practice went by like minutes. Finally, Burke stopped the play and called the team together. "Sit on the floor and let your feet hang down, guys." He spun the basketball on his index finger, then caught it.

Jay knew what was coming: the pep talk. He suddenly felt like a spy. All the fun of playing basketball and the confidence he'd built up during practice evaporated. Burke was about to tell his team they had to smother Richmond Academy in tomorrow's game and there was Jay, a Richmond ex, sitting among them.

"Fluke. That's the key word I want you think about tomorrow afternoon. Fluke. Because that's what it was when the Richmond Rockets snuck that single point past us a few weeks ago. They didn't do it again. And they won't do it again. Who won the MacLeod tournament?"

"We did!" yelled all the guys around Jay. He hadn't expected the cheer and was caught off guard, silent.

"And whose going to win tomorrow?"

"We are!"

Still, Jay was silent. Burke noticed.

How could he yell "We are!" and mean Centreville? He was picturing Tyler and Colin, Coach Willis, and the rest of the guys. Probably they were at practice right now too. Probably Coach Willis was giving them a pep talk about pounding down the Cougar's score and going for a win.

"Anyone want to remind us why we'll win tomorrow?" asked Burke. "Mike?" He tossed the ball and Mike caught it.

Mike stood up and faced his teammates. "Regional champs don't lose. Take a look at those banners up there." Everyone swivelled their heads to check out the large championship banners that lined the gymnasium. "See that empty space? That's where this year's Western Regional Basketball Championship banner's gonna go!"

Everyone thumped his fists in rhythm on the floor, like a drum roll, ending in a cheer for the Cougars. Jay could only watch and listen.

Mike threw the basketball back to Burke.

"Jay, maybe you could give the rest of the guys some kind

of sense of how it's going for you right now. You've had your first practice with us. And you gave us some of your best basketball. No doubt about that, hey guys?"

The team applauded.

"We're gonna be playing Richmond. May as well face that here together so we don't have any hidden agendas when we're on this basketball court tomorrow."

Jay froze where he was sitting. "Um … I'm not sure what to say, sir."

"Off the top of your head. Just anything you're thinking."

"Well … I'm glad I'm playing basketball again." He didn't stand up and he was glad that Burke hadn't thrown the ball to him like he had for Mike. "I love basketball. That's about all I'm thinking right now. It's gonna be weird if I actually get to play tomorrow. I mean, I know all those Richmond guys, and … well … we … they really want to win too. It's like Centreville's the team to beat. You guys're like the number-one opponent."

The team went into that fist drum roll thing and then the cheer. Jay was relieved to be cut off because what else was there to say? Maybe he was at Centreville now, but it still felt too weird. He was hoping with all his might he hadn't made a big mistake.

9

Out of Bounds

S ounds like a perfect plan," Jay heard his mother saying as he walked downstairs to dinner that evening.

"What docs?"

"Your father just said we should all go watch your basketball game tomorrow afternoon. Gramp, Sam, all of us."

"Be like old times, back in that gym," said his father.

"Mr. Burke says I probably won't play, though." Jay wasn't too keen about the plan. It was going to be weird enough being on Centreville's team bench, wearing that red and yellow uniform, without his whole family cheering for the Cougars right in front of his old team.

"Burke'll put you out there. At least give you a feel for your new team."

"It's settled, then. And we'll go for pizza after the game," said his mother.

"I'm buyin'," said Gramp.

Rudy lifted his head off the mat where he lay dozing, and thumped his tail, probably hearing the word "pizza" through the zeds in his dream.

* * *

Jay looked down at the red and yellow uniform he had just put on. He couldn't shake the weird feeling that he was a spy in the Cougars' locker room. The Richmond team would be putting on their white and blue uniforms in the locker room across the hall. Coach Willis would be giving last minute reminders, just like Burke was doing right now.

Mike was standing beside Jay, with one foot up on the bench, tying his sneakers. They were white high-cut sneakers with a triple band of midnight blue, white, and metallic silver that looped up from the side and around the heel. But Mike had substituted thick red laces in place of the white ones.

"What's with the red laces?" said Jay.

"Good luck charm. It works."

Jay thought about the white and blue boxer shorts he used to wear for good luck in the Richmond games. He hoped it wasn't bad luck that they were burned up in the fire, even the two new pairs.

"Hey, did you know that a whole shipload of sneakers like yours got dumped in the ocean?"

Mike stopped tying his laces. "Huh? What're you talking about?"

"Some boat sank a long time ago and it had thousands of sneakers on it and then the sneakers floated all the way up to Alaska. People kept finding them washed up on the shore. Too weird."

"Wouldn't mind finding a pair. Save a pile of cash."

"Trouble is, they'd find one size nine and one size six or something like that. Useless."

"Okay guys!" shouted Burke. "It's show time. Let's get out there and chalk up another victory!"

The Cougars fans cheered as their team jogged out of the locker room. Jay kept his eyes on the guy in front of him. He knew it would only take seconds for his Richmond teammates to notice him wearing Centreville's colors.

"There he is! There's Jay! Right there!" yelled Sam.

Jay glanced into the bleachers. There was Sam sitting between his father and Gramp. His mom was waving frantically. Jay lifted one hand in their direction. It felt as if everyone in the whole place was staring at him. His stomach churned and his concentration was definitely getting messed up.

When the Centreville team made a semi-circle across the top of the key to take a few shots, Jay checked out the white and blue action at the other end of the gym. Just as he did, Colin checked him out. Their eyes sent each other the same one-word message: *Traitor*.

Jay was relieved to be sitting on the bench when the action of the game started. Tyler and Colin were out there on the court. And Barry, Steve, and Philip. Richmond's first line, minus Jay. It was too weird. His mind was humming with questions: What was he doing in a red and yellow uniform? Why was he behind enemy lines? How could things get so complicated so fast?

When a Centreville play added another two points, Jay would get the same sinking feeling he knew the Richmond guys felt. He tried not to let it show, and maybe no one on the Centreville team noticed anyway because they were so into this winning streak.

The game was sloppy all through the first half, with clumsy fouls stacking up on both sides. Mac, eager to move Centreville's ball towards the hoop, slammed into his man in the very first play of the game. Colin was rough under the basket and claimed a couple of fouls for Richmond. Vince scrambled too aggressively after the ball and matched Colin's fouls. If fouls were given for dirty looks, both Vince and Colin would've added even more. Tyler's frustration with Richmond's lagging score showed up in the way he was all over Chris as soon as he had the ball. He fouled Chris once. Chris, feeling crowded (and who would blame him?) elbowed Tyler twice and got caught both times. When a Centreville player violated by stepping inside the paint just as Mike was about to take one of his foul shots, the referee blew the whistle. "Rebounder in too soon." Mike lost his chance to shoot and Centreville's total number of fouls became dangerously close to a bonus situation. Richmond had three fouls against them, but Centreville now had six.

Maybe the Cougars weren't worried about the possibility of a bonus situation. Their score stayed comfortably ahead of Richmond, so what would it matter if Richmond got a free shot if someone fouled against them?

Burke's half-time pep talk was all "Keep Richmond down," and "Take it easy on those aggressive fouls," and "The Rockets already know they've lost this game."

But in the last quarter, with Centreville's score eight points past Richmond's, Burke pulled a big surprise — he put Jay in the game.

His knees felt wobbly as he got up off the bench and jogged across the basketball court to sub in for Chris. They exchanged a quick high five. The other guys on his line were Mike, Alex, Mac, and Vince.

Jay gave a half smile to his new opponent: Tyler. Colin walked behind Tyler and patted him on the back. Tyler smiled at Colin but not at Jay. It was too weird.

Alex was standing out of bounds. The referee looked towards the scorekeepers, pointed to the Richmond hoop, then threw the ball to Alex. In a quick, solid move, Alex made a pass to Vince and the action swept down the outside lane. Tyler's elbow and forearm kept bumping Jay as he attempted to block Jay's forward motion. Jay concentrated on the direction of the ball and tried to remember that he was wearing red and yellow, not white and blue.

Watching Vince move that basketball like his hands were magnets and seeing that the Richmond guard didn't have a chance, Jay's instinct was to move in and try a trap — on Vince, his new teammate! His mind was like the inside of a beehive — all buzzing and chaos. He just couldn't get a clear map of this basketball game.

Suddenly Vince stopped and threw the ball to Jay. Luckily, his hands were on automatic and he caught the pass. Tyler blocked him, but Mike did a well-timed pick and roll. Jay was free. He went in for the lay-up. The basketball slammed against the backboard and sailed back out into Colin's hands.

Colin spun around and ran to the other end of the court with fierce concentration. Centreville's defense didn't catch up. He slammed the ball through the hoop for two points. The Richmond guys swarmed Colin with pats on the back and way-to-go punches.

Jay took a deep, nervous breath. He glanced over in Burke's direction. The coach was standing up and rubbing his hand across his mouth, but he didn't call Jay back to the bench. The time on the clock was 2:19. The score was Centreville 78, Richmond Academy 72.

Even though the score still made a Richmond win seem unlikely, that last basket gave the players in white and blue a blast of new energy. Richmond caught the inbounds pass, but lost the ball on a double dribble. Coach Willis shouted for the guys to slow down, watch the action, stay in the game.

Now Mike was standing out of bounds, holding the ball. In an almost hidden move that might've looked like he was just getting his hair out of his eyes, he gave the three-finger signal. Jay knew this play from yesterday's practice. It meant that Alex would slide backwards to the other side of the court and Vince would stay close to Mike, looking like he was ready to catch the pass. Jay and Mac would be decoys, with a quick start in the direction of the Richmond basket.

The ball spun in a straight line across the court to Alex. His Richmond guard was quickly left behind. Mike ran down center. Colin kept up with him step for step until Mike zigzagged around an invisible barrier and was open for the return pass from Alex. Mike jumped up. Colin was in the air beside him, but his defense failed. The net danced as the ball swished through the hoop. Centreville 80, Richmond 72. Alex gave Mike a high five. Colin gave Jay a dirty look.

Sweat stuck to Jay's hair and forehead. He kept rubbing the palms of his hands on the seat of his shorts. The tension he felt wasn't like anything he'd experienced before. It reminded him of dreaming, when there you are in a place you sort of know but where things are all out of kilter. You're swimming but it isn't water — it's a snowdrift. You're running but your legs aren't taking you anywhere. You're playing basketball but you're wearing the wrong uniform.

There was no time to figure any of this out. The ball was in Tyler's hands and he was heading in the direction of the Centreville basket. Jay kept close, forcing Tyler further into the outside lane, then out of bounds. The referee's whistle blew and Jay had the ball. Tyler waved his arms like a windmill but Jay made the bounce-pass out to Mike.

Mike started down the inside lane in full control of the ball. Jay ran up the outside lane, lost Tyler, and turned to receive Mike's pass. Then Jay meant to make a long pass forward to Vince who was in the short corner, but his arms were robbed of their usual energy. The ball made a slow arc, easily intercepted by a Richmond player who instantly reversed the direction of the game. The ball was immediately passed to Tyler. In the scramble to switch from offense to defense, Jay got too close to Tyler and tripped him. The referee's whistle blew. Jay had fouled against Richmond. Centreville's seventh foul.

Richmond was now in a bonus situation.

Again, Jay looked over at Burke, expecting to get hauled off the floor. But Burke still didn't do that. He was looking up at the scoreboard clock.

Tyler stood at the free throw line to take his single shot. Jay got into position along the key. Tyler aimed short and the ball bounced on the front of the rim. Colin out-jumped Mike for the rebound and leapt right back up for two Richmond points, narrowing the gap to three baskets.

Burke gave the time-out signal and the teams jogged over to their respective coaches. Water bottles were passed around the huddles.

"Take him off the floor, Burke," snapped Vince. "The guy's still playin' for Richmond. That was our seventh foul. He's practically handing points over to those guys."

Jay wasn't expecting that. Sure his head was buzzing and his body wasn't exactly cooperating on all the plays, but no way was he trying to help his old team. "I didn't foul on purpose."

"No? Looked like it to me."

"Hold on. Hold on," said Burke. "I brought you guys off the floor to chill out, not boil over. And by the way, I'm the coach, Vince. I make the calls. If I need your help, I'll write you a letter." He gave Vince a quick silent stare and no one else spoke. "Now hear this. Everyone. There's less than two minutes left in this basketball game. You can go out there and play it like you've already won and let these guys pile up some more cheap points. Or you can be a championship team and get out there and play like every basket is worth a million bucks. It's your call."

The team huddled and shouted, "Cougars rule!"

Jay was jammed in the huddle, but he just couldn't join in the cheer.

Vince noticed. He gave him a sideways look that was a clear warning: Mess up again and you're in trouble. Big time.

Jay took a couple of deep breaths. His stomach still bubbled with tension. He glanced over at the bleachers and saw that Sam was standing up now between his father and Gramp. The little guy seemed just as tense as Jay was.

The clock showed 1:41. An eternity.

Vince took the ball out of bounds. Jay stepped into position, one foot in front of Tyler's. Vince bounced the ball in a sharp angle to Jay, but somehow Tyler grabbed it. When he started to run, he tripped over Jay's left foot and fell. Again. The referee's whistle blasted. Jay had fouled. Again. Richmond had a free throw.

Vince was suddenly in front of Jay, shoving him aggressively. Jay fell backwards across Tyler who managed to get one arm up to protect himself, breaking Jay's fall.

No one was ready for the explosion that followed. Colin appeared out of nowhere with Mike right behind him. Suddenly there was a tangle of white, blue, red and yellow. The ref's whistle was screeching like a siren. But the tangle did not unravel.

Someone's shoulder slammed against Jay and someone else had a fistful of his hair. He just got his hands up in time to protect his face when a white and blue uniform smothered him. The ref's whistle kept blaring.

All this happened in seconds. Then the referees and coaches unravelled the tangle, their firm hands pulling opponents apart.

When he was freed, Jay stood up and turned to offer a hand to Tyler. Tyler gave Jay a dirty look and got up by himself.

Colin was standing close to Mike, his fierce eyes threatening. Coach Willis pulled Colin back to the bench.

"Technical foul for fighting!" shouted the referee. "Centreville 24, Richmond 36, and Centreville 17! These players will leave the gym!"

Centreville 24 was Vince. Richmond 36 was Colin. It took Jay a couple of seconds before he realized who Centreville 17 was — it was him! He couldn't believe it!

10

Courage

Jay went to the Centreville locker room, but he wasn't alone. Vince was right behind him.

"Hope you're satisfied now," sneered Vince.

"Lay off. It's not like you think."

"Oh yeah?"

"Yeah. All I was trying to do is play basketball."

"For Richmond, maybe. Not for us."

"I didn't do anything wrong on purpose. It just happened." He hauled a towel out of his backpack and rubbed the sweat off his face. "You try playing against your old team. It's too weird. Everything's confusing. Everyone's your enemy all of a sudden. Everyone's watching every lousy thing you do."

"Well they must have been watching you big time because all your moves were lousy."

He could see from the look in Vince's eyes that he wanted to continue the fight, right there in the locker room. Red and yellow against red and yellow.

After not playing basketball for two whole weeks, after being forced into watching a game from the bleachers, after going through all the trouble of getting back on the basketball court, where was he now? He was banned from the gym, standing in the locker room facing his new teammate who was also his new enemy.

"You want to know something?" said Jay. "I like basketball more than anything. I didn't ask to move to Centreville. I didn't want to switch basketball teams. I didn't try to mess up out there on that court. And I'll tell you something else. The only way I get to play basketball right now is with the Cougars. So I'm not getting kicked off for fighting someone on my own team."

He took off his uniform and stepped into one of the shower stalls. The heat and rhythm of the water soothed his scrambled mind and washed away the sweat of the game. It was a relief.

Vince was sitting on the bench and Jay was standing beside the shower stall with his towel wrapped around him when the team came into the locker room. But something was wrong. No one was grinning. No one was bragging about any plays. Just about everyone shot Jay a dirty look.

"What's going on?" said Vince.

"We lost."

"Lost! How?"

Jay couldn't believe his ears.

Burke came into the locker room and closed the door firmly behind him. "Take a seat. Everyone."

The coach waited until the room was quiet. "I've got two things to say. First, this is no championship team. You guys folded out there. As soon as Richmond saw your weak point, they had you."

"But—"

"Forget it, Vince. There's no excuse. Especially from you. Your temper cost us big time."

"I wasn't the only one. Jay—"

Burke cut him off again. "That brings me to the second thing I want to say." He turned towards Jay. "All this guy did out there was try to give us the best basketball he could under the circumstances. Both his fouls were unintentional. Anyone could see that. He was rattled. Who wouldn't be rattled in a game you're playing against your old team?"

The coach gazed slowly around the room, silent. No one moved. Some of the guys hung their heads.

"Courage. That's something you know about, Jay. Real courage." Burke walked towards Jay. "I want to shake your hand. I want to congratulate you on your fine show of courage."

Jay hung onto the towel with one hand and accepted the coach's handshake with the other. He knew his face was burning red.

"Because courage is what it took for Jay to come and ask me for a Centreville uniform." Burke started to walk around the locker room, making sure he had the attention of each player. "He had courage when he showed up for practice yesterday and played some excellent basketball. He had courage today when he put on the red and yellow and went out of here with the rest of you guys to face a most unusual situation. Courage."

He turned back to Jay, waited a few seconds, and then said, "I'm proud to have you on our team, Jay."

Then the coach left the locker room.

At first, no one moved. It was like everyone was waiting for someone else to do something. Mike took the hint. He went over to Jay and extended his hand. "Burke's right. Your game was off. But you were working for us. I know it."

Jay accepted the handshake. "Thanks."

The other players snapped out of their daze. One of them said that the ref gave Jay a few tough calls. Another one said, "Even though we lost today, we still have more wins than any team in the league. The Cougars'll still be going to the regionals."

Jay dried himself off and quickly got dressed. He knew his parents and Gramp and Sam would be waiting for him, but there was something he needed to do.

He left the Centreville locker room and crossed the hall.

When he knocked heavily on the door, Tyler opened it. Coach Willis was right behind Tyler.

"Hi, Coach. Um, I gotta say something. I mean to the team."

"Come right on in, my boy." Willis turned and shouted, "Listen up, guys! Jay's here to say something. Listen up!"

"I just wanted to tell you guys that I'm playing basketball for Centreville right now, but … well, it's not like I'm any different than when I played for Richmond. Some of you guys're acting like I'm some kind of enemy." He made sure he didn't look directly at Colin and Tyler. "But I'm not. And I'm not Centreville's enemy either. I'm just playing basketball because I love playing basketball. It's simple."

Coach Willis came up to Jay and gave him a friendly slap on the back. "And you make sure you play your Richmond best in those regionals. Make us proud."

"Yes, sir. If Burke'll put me in the games."

"He will. Don't you doubt that for a minute. He knows a fine ball player when he sees one."

"Coach? Um … what'd you guys win by?"

"A single sweet point. 79–78. Tyler came out from under that pileup when you guys got your fouls. We just couldn't stop him. Scored twice in under a minute. Then Centreville fouled us. Because of the bonus situation, we made the point we needed."

It was Jay's foul that had set up the bonus situation against Centreville. That meant he sort of set up the Richmond win. "I didn't foul on purpose, Coach. I—"

"'Course you didn't foul on purpose. Everyone could see that, even the refs. But that's the way it goes. A game's a game. Rules are rules."

"Right." Jay looked around at the faces of his old teammates. It was obvious they were feeling like champions. And why not? Right now they were champions. "Well, guess I'll get goin'. See ya, Coach. And I'm glad you guys won the game, even though Centreville still gets to go to the regionals. There's always next year. So, well, see you guys."

* * *

Jay sat in the back of the van with Sam and Gramp. He tried to answer every question without blurring any of the facts. Yes, he had been nervous and missed some good plays. No, he didn't trip Tyler on purpose. No, he wasn't too discouraged. Yes, he would stay on the Centreville team.

"It'll be weird, though," he said as the van pulled into the parking lot of Jake's Pizza Place. "It won't feel like I'm really on the championship team. If there's a picture taken, I'll skip it."

Jay saw his mother give that certain look to his father. Gramp reached behind Sam and gave Jay's shoulder a solid squeeze.

Lots of people had the same idea of getting pizza after the game so the place was already full. Three groups were ahead of them waiting for a table as Jay and his family stepped inside.

"Hey, Jay! Over here!" Mike was standing up and waving from a booth where he sat with one other person – someone Jay didn't know. "There's room here. Come on."

Jay walked over. "But there's five of us."

"You'll all fit in. We can put another chair at the end there."

Everyone squeezed around the booth and Gramp sat in the chair. Jay introduced his family to Mike Murphy and Mike introduced his brother, Chad.

"Now, you two fellas are Aubrey Murphy's grandsons, aren't ya?" said Gramp.

"Yes, sir," said Chad.

"Used to fish with Aubrey before I got my own boat. That was some long time ago, mind."

Jay noticed the small Acadia University crest on Chad's T-shirt. "Hey, you go to Acadia?"

"He's on the basketball team," said Mike. "Starting centre."

"I played for them myself," said Jay's dad. "About two decades ago. Jay'll be heading off to Acadia, won't you, Jay?"

"That'll be hundred years from now, Dad."

"Mike's going to Acadia too," said Chad. "You guys'll have no problem making the basketball team. You got the height. You got the moves."

Jay couldn't help but smile. Now he was on Mike's team. Next year, he'd be Mike's opponent again. But if Chad was right, they'd both be wearing Acadia's colours after they finished high school. Maybe they'd even get to play in the nationals. That'd be too cool.

"I'm hungry," said Sam.

"That your stomach growlin'? I thought Rudy must've somehow snuck over to this pizza place and hid right under this table," said Gramp. "Remember everyone, I'm buyin'."

"What can I get you?" asked the waiter, holding a pencil above his notepad, ready to scribble.

"Pepperomi pizza," said Sam.

"Extra large, please. With muchrooms," said his father.

"And how about adding some hangaber too," said his mother.

Mike and Chad looked confused. The waiter hadn't written anything on his notepad.

Jay managed to keep a straight face. "Bet I know exactly what Sam wants to drink," he said. "Boot reer."

Sam burst out laughing.

Mike and Chad finally got the joke.

"You wanna run that by me again?" said the waiter.

* * *

As soon as they were back at Gramp's, Jay went up to his room and straight to the closet. He rummaged through the pile of clothes on the floor until he found what he was looking for underneath. The pennant was a bit bunched up, but the thin stick that supported it hadn't broken.

He went downstairs and into the kitchen. "Anyone got a couple of tacks?"

"What kind of tacks?" asked Gramp.

"Just ordinary tacks. Gotta put something back up on the wall."

"How 'bout small nails? I got lotsa nails."

"Sure. Nails'll be okay."

Jay found the holes in the wallpaper where the tacks had held the pennant for all those years. He was just about to hammer the first nail in when his father came into the room.

"Redecorating?"

"Just putting this back."

"Fell off, eh?"

"Um, no … I threw it in the closet. A couple weeks ago. I was mad."

"And I guess you're not mad now."

"Right."

"Good."

"This how you had it?" Jay adjusted the pennant, tilting it slightly.

"That's about it. Yeah. Right there." Then he said, "Tough first game."

"It was crazy. Geez, I had to keep looking down at my uniform to remember what team I was on!"

"What you did wasn't easy. Lots of people would've just sat out the season."

"I couldn't do that. Basketball's too important. I have to

play. No matter how crazy it is, like with my friends being my opponents, and vice versa." He remembered Colin's dirty look and how Tyler wouldn't accept a hand up after the scramble. He thought of the anger in Vince's eyes when they both were fouled out of the game.

"I was proud to see you out there on that basketball court."

"Even when I messed up?"

"Even when your two feet were running in opposite directions and your eyes were spinning like pin balls."

"How about when my knees were like putty?"

"I was still proud."

"Or when my hands were blobs of jelly?"

"Didn't matter one bit to me. Or your mom, or Gramp, or Sam."

"Thanks, Dad."

* * *

Rudy was still dozing on the sofa when Jay came downstairs, unable to sleep and thinking of watching something on Gramp's lame TV. Everyone else was in bed.

He went into the kitchen and poured a tall glass of milk. Then he smeared peanut butter on a slice of bread and folded it over. That first bite through the bubble of peanut butter and bread was the best.

The news was on one channel and a movie from the last century was on the only other channel. Better than nothing.

Jay sat beside Rudy, who didn't move. He put his feet up on the coffee table next to the newspaper and a small stack of flyers. He polished off most of the sandwich and gulped the milk. Rudy lifted his head and sniffed. Jay gave him a corner of bread and peanut butter. He was sure that Rudy smiled.

Jay thought about the courage speech that Burke delivered to the Centreville team. All through the game, and even when he was putting on his uniform before it started, he had hardly been able to concentrate. He had been so confused. Even afraid. And then Burke talks about how he has all this courage. That was weird. But maybe it actually made sense in a way. If a person did things when they weren't afraid, then who'd bother saying anything about courage?

He wondered if the guys on the Centreville team, or even on the Richmond team, would see things the way Burke did. Maybe it didn't even matter.

Next year, Jay would be back at Richmond Academy. It wouldn't be the same. But it wouldn't be much different either. People would forget about some stuff and remember other stuff. He was figuring it would be like going to any school: playing basketball was the main reason to be there.

Beside the newspaper on the coffee table was a flyer for Harmon's Men's Wear. Jay picked it up and flipped to the under-wear section.

Other books you'll enjoy in the Sports Stories series...

Baseball

❏ *Curve Ball* by John Danakas #1
Tom Poulos is looking forward to a summer of baseball in Toronto until his mother puts him on a plane to Winnipeg.

❏ *Baseball Crazy* by Martyn Godfrey #10
Rob Carter wins an all-expenses-paid chance to be bat boy at the Blue Jays spring training camp in Florida.

❏ *Shark Attack* by Judi Peers #25
The East City Sharks have a good chance of winning the county championship until their archrivals get a tough new pitcher.

❏ *Hit and Run* by Dawn Hunter and Karen Hunter #35
Glen Thomson is a talented pitcher, but as his ego inflates, team morale plummets. Will he learn from being benched for losing his temper?

❏ *Power Hitter* by C. A. Forsyth #41
Connor's summer was looking like a write-off. That is, until he discovered his secret talent.

❏ *Sayonara, Sharks* by Judi Peers #48
In this sequel to *Shark Attack*, Ben and Kate are excited about the school trip to Japan, but Matt's not sure he wants to go.

Basketball

❏ *Fast Break* by Michael Coldwell #8
Moving from Toronto to small-town Nova Scotia was rough, but when Jeff makes the school basketball team he thinks things are looking up.

❏ *Camp All-Star* by Michael Coldwell #12
In this insider's view of a basketball camp, Jeff Lang encounters some unexpected challenges.

❏ *Nothing but Net* by Michael Coldwell #18
The Cape Breton Grizzly Bears prepare for an out-of-town basketball tournament they're sure to lose.

❏ *Slam Dunk* by Steven Barwin and Gabriel David Tick #23
In this sequel to *Roller Hockey Blues*, Mason Ashbury's basketball team
adjusts to the arrival of some new players: girls.

❏ *Courage on the Line* by Cynthia Bates #33
After Amelie changes schools, she must confront difficult former teammates in an extramural match.

❏ *Free Throw* by Jacqueline Guest #34
Matthew Eagletail must adjust to a new school, a new team and a new
father along with five pesky sisters.

❏ *Triple Threat* by Jacqueline Guest #38
Matthew's cyber-pal Free Throw comes to visit, and together they face a
bully on the court.

❏ *Queen of the Court* by Michele Martin Bossley #40
What happens when the school's fashion queen winds up on the basketball court?

❏ *Shooting Star* by Cynthia Bates #46
Quyen is dealing with a troublesome teammate on her new basketball
team, as well as trouble at home. Her parents seem haunted by something
that happened in Vietnam.

❏ *Home Court Advantage* by Sandra Diersch #51
Debbie had given up hope of being adopted, until the Lowells came along.
Things were looking up, until Debbie is accused of stealing from the team.

❏ *Rebound* by Adrienne Mercer #54
C.J.'s dream in life is to play on the national basketball team. But one day she
wakes up in pain and can barely move her joints, much less be a star player.

❏ *Out of Bounds* by Sylvia Gunnery # 70
When the Hirtle family's house burns down, Jay is forced to relocate and
switch schools. He has a choice: sacrifice a year of basketball or play on
the same team as his archrival Mike.

Figure Skating

❏ *A Stroke of Luck* by Kathryn Ellis #6
Strange accidents are stalking one of the skaters at the Millwood Arena.

❏ *The Winning Edge* by Michele Martin Bossley #28
Jennie wants more than anything to win a gruelling series of competitions, but is success worth losing her friends?

❏ *Leap of Faith* by Michele Martin Bossley #36
Amy wants to win at any cost, until an injury makes skating almost impossible. Will she go on?

Gymnastics

❏ *The Perfect Gymnast* by Michele Martin Bossley #9
Abby's new friend has all the confidence she needs, but she also has a serious problem that nobody but Abby seems to know about.

Ice Hockey

❏ *Two Minutes for Roughing* by Joseph Romain #2
As a new player on a tough Toronto hockey team, Les must fight to fit in.

❏ *Hockey Night in Transcona* by John Danakas #7
Cody Powell gets promoted to the Transcona Sharks' first line, bumping out the coach's son, who's not happy with the change.

❏ *Face Off* by C. A. Forsyth #13
A talented hockey player finds himself competing with his best friend for a spot on a select team.

❏ *Hat Trick* by Jacqueline Guest #20
The only girl on an all-boy hockey team works to earn the captain's respect and her mother's approval.

❏ *Hockey Heroes* by John Danakas #22
A left-winger on the thirteen-year-old Transcona Sharks adjusts to a new best friend and his mom's boyfriend.

❏ *Hockey Heat Wave* by C. A. Forsyth #27
In this sequel to *Face Off*, Zack and Mitch run into trouble when it looks as if only one of them will make the select team at hockey camp.

❑ *Shoot to Score* by Sandra Richmond #31
Playing defense on the B list alongside the coach's mean-spirited son is a tough obstacle for Steven to overcome, but he perseveres and changes his luck.

❑ *Rookie Season* by Jacqueline Guest #42
What happens when a boy wants to join an all-girl hockey team?

❑ *Brothers on Ice* by John Danakas #44
Brothers Dylan and Deke both want to play goal for the same team.

❑ *Rink Rivals* by Jacqueline Guest #49
A move to Calgary finds the Evans twins pitted against each other on the ice, and struggling to help each other out of trouble.

❑ *Power Play* by Michele Martin Bossley #50
An early-season injury causes Zach Thomas to play timidly, and a school bully just makes matters worse. Will a famous hockey player be able to help Zach sort things out?

❑ *Danger Zone* by Michele Martin Bossley #56
When Jason accidentally checks a player from behind, the boy is seriously hurt. Jason is devastated when the boy's parents want him suspended from the league.

❑ *Ice Attack* by Beatrice Vandervelde #58
Alex and Bill used to be an unbeatable combination on the Lakers hockey team. Now that they are enemies, Alex is thinking about quitting.

❑ *Red-Line Blues* by Camilla Reghelini Rivers #59
Lee's hockey coach is only interested in the hotshots on his team. Ordinary players like him spend their time warming the bench.

❑ *Goon Squad* by Michele Martin Bossley #63
Jason knows he shouldn't play dirty, but the coach of his hockey team is telling him otherwise. This book is the exciting follow-up to *Power Play* and *Danger Zone*.

❏ *Ice Dreams* by Beverly Scudamore #65
Twelve-year-old Maya is a talented figure skater, just as her mother was before she died four years ago. Despite pressure from her family to keep skating, Maya tries to pursue her passion for goaltending.

Riding
❏ *A Way with Horses* by Peter McPhee #11
A young Alberta rider, invited to study show jumping at a posh local riding school, uncovers a secret.

❏ *Riding Scared* by Marion Crook #15
A reluctant new rider struggles to overcome her fear of horses.

❏ *Katie's Midnight Ride* by C. A. Forsyth #16
An ambitious barrel racer finds herself without a horse weeks before her biggest rodeo.

❏ *Glory Ride* by Tamara L. Williams #21
Chloe Anderson fights memories of a tragic fall for a place on the Ontario Young Riders Team.

❏ *Cutting It Close* by Marion Crook #24
In this novel about barrel racing, a young rider finds her horse is in trouble just as she's about to compete in an important event.

❏ *Shadow Ride* by Tamara L. Williams #37
Bronwen has to choose between competing aggressively for herself or helping out a teammate.

Roller Hockey
❏ *Roller Hockey Blues* by Steven Barwin and Gabriel David Tick #17
Mason Ashbury faces a summer of boredom until he makes the roller hockey team.

Running
❏ *Fast Finish* by Bill Swan #30
Noah is a promising young runner headed for the provincial finals when he suddenly decides to withdraw from the event.

Soccer

❏ *Lizzie's Soccer Showdown* by John Danakas #3
When Lizzie asks why the boys and girls can't play together, she finds herself the new captain of the soccer team.

❏ *Alecia's Challenge* by Sandra Diersch #32
Thirteen-year-old Alecia has to cope with a new school, a new step-father, and friends who have suddenly discovered the opposite sex.

❏ *Shut-Out!* by Camilla Reghelini Rivers #39
David wants to play soccer more than anything, but will the new coach let him?

❏ *Offside!* by Sandra Diersch #43
Alecia has to confront a new girl who drives her teammates crazy.

❏ *Heads Up!* by Dawn Hunter and Karen Hunter #45
Do the Warriors really need a new, hot-shot player who skips practice?

❏ *Off the Wall* by Camilla Reghelini Rivers #52
Lizzie loves indoor soccer, and she's thrilled when her little sister gets into the sport. But when their teams are pitted against each other, Lizzie can only warn her sister to watch out.

❏ *Trapped!* by Michele Martin Bossley #53
There's a thief on Jane's soccer team, and everyone thinks it's her best friend, Ashley. Jane must find the true culprit to save both Ashley and the team's morale.

❏ *Soccer Star!* by Jacqueline Guest #61
Samantha longs to show up Carly, the school's reigning soccer star, but her new interest in theatre is taking up a lot of her time. Can she really do it all?

❏ *Miss Little's Losers* by Robert Rayner #64
The Brunswick Valley School soccer team haven't won a game all season long. When their coach resigns, the only person who will coach them is Miss Little … their former kindergarten teacher!